I0769541

Pumpkin to Talk About

A NOVELLA

ALLIE SAMBERTS

Copyright © 2024 by Allie Samberts

ISBN: 979-8-9878241-6-0 (paperback)

All rights reserved.

No portion of this book may be reproduced in any form or by any electronic or mechanical means, including information storage and retrieval systems, without written permission from the author, except for the use of brief quotations in a book review, and except as permitted by U.S. copyright law.

This is a work of fiction. Names, characters, places, and incidents either are the product of the author's imagination or are used fictitiously. Any resemblance to actual persons, living or dead, events, or locales is entirely coincidental.

Cover Design by Lorissa Padilla

Chapter Art by Lorissa Padilla

alliesambertswrites@gmail.com

www.alliesamberts.com

For Team Mike.

Thanks for ~~pushing~~ supporting me.

Author's Note

Anyone who knows me knows that Halloween is one of my least favorite holidays. Which is probably why it never occurred to me to write a Halloween book. I don't like being scared, and I'm not particularly fond of costumes or parties. But, when I was sitting here one day, bored and wondering what to write next, someone in my writing group jokingly said, "Write a Halloween novella!" And thus, this book was born.

Writing this book was such a joy. I know I say that about all of my books, but I truly mean it about this one. I wrote it so quickly—partially because I was working with pre-formed characters, and partially because I gave myself a challenge to see if I could meet it. There was no room for imposter syndrome or self-doubt like there is with longer projects. I had only a few weeks to put this together, so I couldn't let anything get in the way.

This may also be the coziest romance I've ever written. I've tried to think of content warnings to include here, and aside from one of the main characters getting teased about being different when she was younger, and a side character dealing with a divorce, I don't think there's much in here that could be concerning.

However, my characters do curse, drink, and have adult relationships. Chapters ten and thirteen contain explicit scenes that are intended for mature audiences only. You can read them or avoid them as you see fit.

And, finally, as you may have guessed from the dedication, Mike is a character I've written about before. He arguably stole the show in my last book, *Common Grounds*. This novella is more of a spinoff than an interconnected standalone, so it can be read independently, but if you want to check out *Common Grounds* first (or if you fall in love with Mike here and want to see more of him later), *Common Grounds* is available on Kindle Unlimited or in paperback wherever books are sold.

Whether you're a fan of spooky season or not, I hope you enjoy your time in Ironwood Flats. Grab some pumpkin bread and settle in for this short, cozy, Halloween book.

CHAPTER 1

MIKE

As soon as I exit the airplane into the terminal of the airport in Austin, I notice three things: the smell of smoked meat from the barbeque stand, the absolute swagger of every single man in the place, and a pop-up shop offering t-shirts emblazoned with *I HEART TEXAS* across the chest where the heart is either colored with the Texas flag or is replaced by the literal state outline.

Pausing to take in a deep breath, I savor the barbeque scent. It's good to be back in the land of ten-gallon hats and twenty-gallon belt buckles.

People from Texas fucking *love* Texas.

Except me, that is. It'll likely only take the hour-long drive from the airport to my hometown of Ironwood Flats—population 18,368—for me to remember exactly why I left. I took a one-way ticket to college in Indiana, jumped on a tech startup with a buddy I met there, settled in the midsized city of Baker's Grove, and never looked back.

Until now, I guess. When my baby sister, Annie, called to tell me she had finally kicked out her good-for-nothing husband and asked me to come help with her two kids, I took a leave of absence from my job and got on a plane as soon as I could.

It's not that I've never been back to Ironwood Flats. I've come back for holidays as much as I can in the twenty-some years I've been away. But this time, my bags are packed for an extended stay. There's no telling how long Annie will need me, and when she calls, I answer. Every single time.

Annie is the youngest of the five Page siblings, and she's always been everyone's favorite. I'm stuck right in the middle, but because I was the only boy, I was showered with attention from all sides. Our oldest sisters—twins Lindsey and Lisa—took it upon themselves to show me and my two younger sisters—Erica and Annie—the ropes. But Lindsey, Lisa, and Erica all did exactly what I did. What most people in our small town did, actually. They went to college and stayed gone. In my sisters' case, they married out-of-towners and had kids. Now, they're scattered like tumbleweeds across the country.

Annie, however, married her high school sweetheart and the quarterback of the school football team, Jacob Adams. The man is insufferable. Every time I'm home, he locks me in his trophy room and more or less forces me to smoke a cigar with him while he relives his glory days, and the women clean up from the meal. Good riddance.

As the only single and child-free member of the Page clan, it's no wonder Annie called me instead of our sisters. I'm more mobile than the others, and why wouldn't I help her out? She's family, after all. Even if it means facing the small town I left behind the minute I graduated high school.

Like clockwork, about thirty minutes into my drive in the rental car I picked up from the airport, I'm starting to feel antsy. The rolling landscape of Texas Hill Country is different than the absolute pancake-flat topography of Indiana, but it does nothing to soothe the jittery feeling I always get when I come back here. I had a lot of friends, but I never felt like I fit in here. I didn't play football, for one, and my love of all things Texas only goes so deep.

When I finally pull into the driveway of Annie's ranch-style home on the edge of town, I take a minute to study the exterior. The paint is chipping, and the front porch has seen better days. One of the shutters hangs loose on the window to the far right of the house, and they're all faded from the scorching Texas sun. The trees here are still a vibrant green, though a few are starting to yellow in the mid-October fall, unlike in Indiana. It was a full foliage fest there when I left. But the bushes haven't been maintained, and the landscaping is more desert-chic than lush oasis. It looks like Jacob hadn't lifted a finger in years to help maintain this place. Figures.

I don't have time to dwell on it, though, because the front door bursts open, and Annie's two kids come running out, barefoot and in mismatched pajamas. I check the clock to see that it's one in the afternoon. Things might be worse off than I thought.

"Uncle Mike!" Nicholas yells, his still-squeaky, ten-year-old voice muffled by the car. "You're here!"

"Best. Day. *Ever!*" Claire pauses in her sprint to clench her fists and yell the last word up into the big, blue, Texas sky.

I can't help but chuckle as I open my door and swing my legs out of the car. Nicholas doesn't even let me stand up; he barrels into me for a hug, pushing me backward. My spine hits the center console with a thud as he practically climbs on top of me.

"Woah there, slugger. It's good to see you, too," I say once I get my breath back. "Where's your mom?"

Nicholas climbs off of me and slouches his shoulders forward a bit. "She's got a headache," he says to the ground. But then he puffs his chest out with obvious pride. "She says I'm the man of the house now."

I ruffle his dark hair, which I also notice is a little long around the ears. "Well, that's true. Does that mean you're doing a good job taking care of your baby sister?"

"I'm not a baby!" Claire protests with a stomp of her foot. "I'm eight!"

"What?" I shout with mock-incredulousness. "Last time I checked, you were six."

In a move so much like her mother, she rolls her eyes dramatically and tips her face upward. "Uncle Mike." She draws out my name in exasperation. "Come on."

"Okay, okay," I concede. "I'm sorry."

"Are you here to help us decorate for Halloween?" Nicholas grunts as he tries to lift my heavy suitcase from the backseat.

"I got that, my man." I take the handle from him, and he looks relieved that I came to his rescue. I try not to groan at his request. I hate Halloween—especially the way this town treats it like the most important celebration in the world. "And... sure. I can help you decorate for Halloween." Among other things that need to be done to this house. If it makes the kids happy, I suppose I can suck it up.

"You can help us with our costumes, too!" Claire jumps up and down behind me as I wheel my suitcase to the porch. The steps up to the front door are, in fact, a death trap.

"Mom said she's going to throw sheets over us, and we can ghost her like Dad did," Nicholas says in the matter-of-fact way of a kid who is quoting words he doesn't fully understand.

We cross the threshold into the house, and I tick an eyebrow up. "She must not give a sheet if she's saying stuff like that," I mumble as I take in the clutter and dust in the living room to my right. There's a clear line of sight to a sink full of dishes in the kitchen.

Claire giggles. "Uncle Mike needs to add a quarter to the swear jar!"

She squeals as I pick her up, tickling her sides. "I said 'sheet,' you little rat!"

"It's... the intent... that matters..." she says between breathless laughter.

I tickle her harder. "You sound like your mom."

Speaking of the devil, a robe-clad Annie appears in the doorway to the kitchen. Her bottle-dyed blonde hair is matted, and she rubs at bleary, blood-shot eyes. "Can you two keep it down?" she moans. Without looking at us, she takes a glass down from a cupboard, fills it with water at the sink, chugs it, and drops it in with the rest of the dirty dishes. A pan clatters to the floor, and she just leaves it there.

Nicholas winces. "There's three of us, Mom," he says. "Uncle Mike is here."

Annie finally looks at me, blinking rapidly. Suddenly, her shoulders slump, and she buries her face in her hands as her body convulses with sobs.

"Oh, shit." I do, actually, curse that time, but a wide-eyed Claire doesn't correct me. In four steps, I cross the threshold and wrap my arms around my little sister. She grips my shirt with her slim hands—have they gotten thinner since the last time I saw her?—and bawls her eyes out.

"It's okay," I croon as I rub her back. "I've got you. We'll get you back on your feet in no time."

"I don't even have a job," she wails into my chest. "What am I going to do?"

"One step at a time, Annie." I look over her head at the clutter. "The first one is to get this place in working order. Kids, time for some chores. I want your rooms cleaned and your toys picked up from the living room. Whoever can do it the fastest wins ice cream after dinner tonight."

Those kids take off at lightning speed, their heavy footsteps sounding throughout the whole house. Annie's sobs have lightened, though she surreptitiously rubs her snotty nose on the fabric of my t-shirt.

"Fuck, Annie. That's so gross," I groan.

"That's fifty cents!" Nicholas cries from his room.

"Dammit," I curse under my breath. I'm going to have to find several rolls of quarters.

"Seventy-five," Annie sniffles, then sighs into me. "I'm so glad you're here."

"Me too," I say, and it's true. I'd go to the ends of the Earth to help my baby sister out of a tough spot. But the walls of this tiny town are already closing in on me, and I hope I can get her back on her feet quickly so I can get out of here and back to my life in the Midwest.

CHAPTER 2

BELLE

MY BOSS'S TERRIBLE HALLOWEEN playlist crackles through the shitty bar speakers. As if the songs from horror movie soundtracks weren't bad enough, they keep going in and out like they're being played from an ancient record player rather than the MP3 player hooked up to the AUX cable behind the bar.

To be fair, that thing is from the early aughts, so an ancient record player might actually work better.

I jiggle the cord until I get consistent sound, then back away slowly so as not to upset the delicate balance. Old Man Peña gives an affirming nod and a grunt from his barstool at the far corner before shaking his empty beer bottle in my direction. I pop the top off another and slide it down the bar into his gnarled, cupped hand. He nods again before taking a drink.

And this is why I love tending bar at The Broken Spur. The weeknight townies are familiar enough that I don't even have to talk to them anymore. It's mostly just me, the horror movie soundtrack, and my thoughts.

But because the universe has it out for me, the door to the bar bursts open and a gaggle of men spill in from the street. A *loud* gaggle at that. There are about ten of them, and they're all pounding each other on the back and shouting in a competition to be heard. I almost turn up the music, but I'm not sure which sound is worse. And I'm pretty sure if the music gets louder, they'll just match it anyway.

I recognize about half of the guys from high school, which is saying something because my twenty-year reunion has just come and gone. I didn't go. I see enough of these assholes here; I didn't need to see them *again* in the Ironwood High School gymnasium while we all pretended to have amounted to something. They've made it clear that they think they're better than me, but we're all stuck here in the same small town we grew up in which puts us on a pretty even playing field as far as I'm concerned.

As if to illustrate this point, Brian Turner saunters up to the bar and leans sloppily against it to look down his nose at me. Even in the musty air of the bar, I can smell the booze rolling off of him. This is clearly not these guys' first stop. He drags his eyes over me, and I have to fight the urge to audibly gag. He is a paying customer, after all, and the owner, Carter, would be none too happy if I pissed them off.

"Hey darlin'," Brian drawls. "Can we get a round of shots for me and my friends here?"

I plaster on a smile that doesn't reach my eyes. "Sure thing. Any particular kind of shot y'all are looking for?"

He licks his lips, and at that, I do shudder. Luckily, he doesn't seem to notice. "Surprise us," he sneers. He leaves his credit card on the bar and makes his way back to his friends.

I take a bottle of tequila off the bottommost shelf and line up ten shot glasses on the bar. I dole out the liquor, drop a bowl of lime wedges and a couple of saltshakers next to them for good measure, then punch in the top shelf tequila price before charging Brian's card. They're too drunk to care how much their shots cost, and it feels like a small win. They surely won't be tipping much, anyway.

They all come over to the bar to grab their tequila. Before they toss them back, they all raise their tiny glasses and shout, "To freedom!" Brian slaps one of the guys on the back—Jacob Adams, I think, though he's looking a lot worse for the wear than the last time he was in here, and it's dark so it's hard to say for sure. Every one of them grimaces when they take their shots. Only two bother with the lime wedges. The rest try to man through it with a few coughs and breaths sucked in between their teeth. I start handing out beer chasers, which Brian also puts on his card. When they finally move to the far side of the bar, I can breathe a little easier again.

I start to wipe up the tequila I spilled while pouring the shots. I've just about finished when the door opens again. This time, only one man walks in, but he turns back to shut the door before I can get a look at his face. All I can see are broad shoulders that test the limits of his collared shirt, and very expensive jeans that hug an excellent ass. I'm sure I've never seen this man before. I'd remember an ass like that.

Except, when he turns back around toward the bar, I get to see his face. The universe really does have it out for me tonight, because I'm met with the high cheekbones, chocolate-brown eyes, and pearly-white smile of none other than Mike Page, my high school nemesis.

What the fuck is he doing here? The last I heard, he hightailed it out of here for college in Indiana and stayed there. Which was all the same to me at the time. Good-fucking-riddance to bad rubbish.

For a moment, I think he might not recognize me. I've changed a lot since the last time he saw me during our senior year of high school. My hair is darker now; I dye it raven-black every few weeks. And I have lots more piercings than I did then. A couple more in my ears, but also one in my nose. I wear dark lipstick, partly because I like it, and partly because of the season. And I've replaced the spaghetti strap tank tops and wide-legged jeans of the 2000s with black leggings, combat boots, and a dark gray off-the-shoulder shirt that shows off my bluebell tattoo.

But he studies me for a moment, and his grin stretches farther across his face. It creases the edges of his mouth which—cruelly—makes him even more attractive. The other guys shout something incomprehensible from their end of the room. Mike eyes them, and his smile falters ever so slightly. When he turns back to me, though, he takes a few strides over to the bar and slides into the stool right in front of me.

"Well, well, well," I say as I continue to wipe off the already-clean bar. "Look what the cat dragged in."

"If it isn't Bonnie Bluebell Allen, as I live and breathe," he says. His voice may be as smooth as butter, but I sneer at the nickname. I haven't heard that one in years. Not since he was tugging at my braids on the playground and taunting me with it.

Even when he kissed me in high school—behind the bleachers like some kind of fucking cliché—my name, Belle, rolled off his tongue in a breathless moan before his lips met mine.

It was the best kiss I ever had. Until I saw him the next day, canoodling Stacey Villarreal, one of the senior cheerleaders. I avoided him as best I could after that. Until now, I guess.

Two can play that game. I'm not the same, timid little girl he used to pick on. "The prodigal son returns," I intone. "Welcome back, Indiana."

"Indiana?" He raises his eyebrows in question. "As in the ruggedly handsome archaeologist?"

I cough out a harsh laugh. "No, as in the place you moved to. Everyone calls you that."

"They do not," he scoffs.

Brian sidles back up to the bar, even sloppier than he was just a few minutes ago. He shoves Mike in the shoulder, and if I didn't know any better, I'd think Mike was about to murder him by the way his dark eyes go almost black with rage.

"Hey, Indiana's back!" Brian yells to his cronies at the back of the room. They return a half-hearted greeting.

Mike's eyes soften a bit as they meet mine. I give him an I-told-you-so shrug before he breaks eye contact with me to glare at Brian's hand, still resting on his shoulder.

"Kindly remove your hand," Mike says through gritted teeth.

Brian does no such thing. He, in fact, leans in closer. The air vibrates between the three of us, and I can almost *feel* Mike about ready to lose his shit. As much as I want to see that, I also don't need the police here tonight over a bar fight, so I chime in.

"Need another round, Brian?" I ask sweetly. That about does it. He turns his attention to me and drops his hand from Mike's shoulder.

"Nah, hun," he slurs. I almost gag again. "I need to close my tab. We're getting out of here. The vibe has changed." He eyes Mike sidelong. Mike, to his credit, is staring at his clasped hands on top of the bar. Sure enough, the rest of his crew loudly scrapes their chairs against the floor as they stand and get ready to leave.

"Oh, you're good," I say. "I didn't leave your tab open."

"Fantastic. Thanks, sweetheart." Brian turns on his heel and follows his friends out the door.

I manage to wait until the door has shut behind him before I give a full-body shudder. "Gross," I mutter before giving Mike my attention again. "What the fuck was that about?"

Mike looks up at me, his expression carefully neutral. "Can I get a whiskey shot and a beer, please? Whatever's on tap."

"Uh, sure." I pour the shot first, and he doesn't even wait for me to pull the beer before he throws it back, the long column of his throat working against the liquid. He slams the shot glass on the top of the bar and hums. I place his pint glass in front of him, then go to clear off the table the guys left behind. By the time I make it back to the bar, Mike looks a lot less bothered. In fact, he seems almost apologetic when he winces up at me.

"Didn't mean to cause a scene," he says quietly.

"You didn't," I assure him. But if there's one thing I've learned in my decade as a bartender here, it's the tells people have when they still have more they want to get off their chests. Mike doesn't seem like he wants to make the first move, though, so I start with some small talk.

"So, how long you in town for?"

He blows out a long puff of air and takes a sip of beer. He puts the glass back on the counter carefully, then runs his finger up and down the condensation on the side. "I'm staying with my sister for a while," he evades.

"Annie?" I ask. Annie was a few years younger than us in school, but she was a spitfire if I ever saw one. Still is, if her high hair and even higher heels when she drops her kids off at school are any indication.

"Yeah," Mike says. He tips his head back to where the guys had been sitting. "You know Jacob Adams? He was in here with those assholes a few minutes ago?"

I nod. "Mmm-hmm." Best not to say too much to someone who is trying to work through some shit.

"She kicked him out. She… uh… well, she's not taking it too well. I'm here to help her out until she can get back on her feet."

Suddenly, the toast to freedom makes sense. It's a small town, but sometimes news doesn't travel as fast as in the movies. Either that, or this is a recent development. "Oh, shit. I'm sorry to hear that. What about the kids?" By day, I'm the elementary school librarian, so every kid in town passes by my desk at least once a week. Nicholas and Claire are voracious readers.

Mike shrugs. "They're with Annie for now. He doesn't seem too interested in them."

Based on what I saw tonight—and the fact that he's never the one at drop off—that checks out. I shake my head in dismay, gazing back at where Jacob had been sitting. I knew there was something about those idiots I didn't like. "That fucker is so low, you couldn't put a rug under him."

To my surprise, Mike barks out a laugh. My gaze slides back to him as he coughs and pounds a fist against his chest. "God damn, Bonnie Belle. You are so fucking *Texan*."

I scoff at him and rub at an invisible spot on the bar top. "Don't forget, you came from here too, Indy."

He hums as he sips his beer again. "I've been gone longer than I ever lived here," he points out. "Long enough to earn that stupid nickname."

I tip my head to concede. He's right. Which makes him just another small-town boy turned big-city man who ran away as if this place was on fire. If that self-satisfied smirk is any indication, he probably never even stops to appreciate his humble roots. I'm sure he'll stay just long enough to make sure Annie is okay, then he'll hightail it out of here and forget about us all over again.

Just as well, I think as I get Old Man Peña another beer. I certainly don't need Mike Page, the boy who terrorized me all through school, back in my life for one minute longer than necessary. No matter how good-looking he is now.

CHAPTER 3

MIKE

THE AIR MATTRESS I found in Annie's closet must have a tiny hole in it. By about five in the morning, my ass is basically on the floor, and my neck is bent at such a weird angle that I'm not sure if it'll ever be straight again.

This is not going to work for any length of time, that's for sure.

But even that's not exactly why I can't sleep. I hate to admit it, but Belle's blue-violet eyes float in and out of my consciousness every time I start to drift off. I was surprised to see her at The Broken Spur. I hadn't seen or heard from her after that kiss we shared behind the bleachers. It was almost like she had disappeared. And then no one has said much about her at all since I left Ironwood Flats, so I kind of assumed she had fled like the rest of us. High school hadn't been kind to her, and most of the people for whom that was the case left at the first chance they got.

Not Belle, though. She must have stuck it out. Or left and come back. I wonder why. The way I remember it, she was always the odd one out in a lot of ways. Her emotions ran wild, and she was unpredictable. Her dark hair kept getting darker and darker with each application of dye, and her makeup and clothing started to match. On top if it all, she was a bit of a loner, which is difficult when your graduating class has two hundred kids, all of whom you've gone to school with since you were in kindergarten.

Of course, when I say high school was not kind to her, I know I played a part in that. Twenty or so years removed from it, I can recognize that I wasn't the best of kids. I was so desperate to fit in that anyone who seemed like they marched to the beat of their own drummer got mocked by my friends and me. She wasn't special in that regard, but I'm sure it hurt, nonetheless. Even though her eyes haunted me then as much then as they do now. And that kiss...

The vinyl of the air mattress makes a swishing noise as I shake my head to clear it. That was over two decades ago. I'm sure she's forgotten about it by now.

She seemed pretty well adjusted when I talked to her last night. Not that I had her attention for all that long. I had just needed something to take the edge off seeing Annie in a heap in her bed for most of the afternoon, so I drank my one beer and left. But I did make sure to drop a generous tip. Partly because my mama raised me right, and partly because I wanted to signal that I've changed since high school.

Laying awake, tossing and turning on the floor of Annie's home-office-slash-nail-studio, those blue-violet eyes flash in my memory again. I hadn't thought about her eyes in a long time, but they're just as stunning now as they were then. And the rest of her... fuck. Regardless of how she's spent her time since high school, she's grown curves in all the right places. And that tattoo on her shoulder. I'm semi-hard just thinking about it.

But here I am, pretending like she didn't spend half the night glaring at me and the other half avoiding eye contact. And who am I kidding? It doesn't matter anyway. I'm not trying to cause even more trouble for myself by seducing Bluebell Allen and then going on my merry way back to Baker's Grove, no matter how much I want to drag my tongue over the petals of the bluebells on her shoulder. I've got enough issues with Annie as it is. I certainly don't need to add more to my plate.

Groaning, I try to sit up. It takes a few tries to work with the deflating mattress in order to get me up, and I eventually end up just rolling off of it onto the floor and standing up from there. Thank god no one was there to see that, because I'd never live it down.

Saturday at five-thirty in the morning. If things haven't changed—and they probably haven't—I know Cathy Johnson opens the café downtown at six on weekends, and Mr. Lewis opens the local hardware store at seven. Maybe I can at least get some caffeine and a jump-start on some of the home improvement projects that need to get done around here.

I pull on an old shirt and some sweatpants, put a backwards hat over my messy hair, hastily brush my teeth, and grab the keys to Annie's truck.

But when I pull up to the café to see new, later hours and an Under New Management sign, I drag my hand over my undercaffeinated face. As if to add insult to injury, the sign is being held by a grinning plastic skeleton inside the window, and it's all illuminated by orange and purple fairy lights.

This is going to be even harder than I thought.

***

Thankfully, Mr. Lewis hasn't changed one single thing since I was in high school. He unlocks the doors promptly at seven, and I stroll in with forced nonchalance, as if I hadn't been sitting in the parking lot doomscrolling on my phone for the past hour.

The building is a flat rectangle that stands alone about a five-minute walk from downtown. The brick is painted yellow and green with *Lewis Hardware* in bold letters above the second story windows. Sunshine and rain have, over the years, weathered the paint and poked holes in the striped awning above the doorway, but it still mostly looks exactly as I remember it. I used to come here with my dad as a kid. He taught me everything I know about power tools—which is, admittedly, not as much as he knows. But he and Mama retired to Florida a few years ago, mostly to be closer to Lindsey when she had her babies. They loved it so much that they stayed, even though her kids are in high school now.

That's okay. This ain't my first rodeo, as he would say. I can fix up Annie's place by Halloween, and hopefully get her back on her feet, too. She'd be embarrassed if our parents knew how low she was feeling, so I make a promise to myself that I'm going to take care of everything for her without dragging them into it.

I take my time perusing the aisles and collecting things I need. Wood and nails for the porch steps, paint for the shutters. I see a sale on dish soap at an endcap and grab that, too. My skin stretches raw across my knuckles, and I wince at the memory of doing all of her dishes yesterday. I toss in a couple pairs of rubber gloves for good measure.

As I'm walking down one of the aisles, pondering how not one single thing has changed in this place over the years, I hear a soft curse from the aisle over. Next thing I know, an entire stack of tall two-by-fours clatters to the ground. Through the open shelving, I can now see bottle-black hair, sparkling jewelry, and those blue-violet eyes that kept me up all night.

Belle doesn't notice me as she puts her hands on her hips and looks at the mess she's made of the wood. She puffs out her cheeks and lets out a slow breath through pursed lips.

"Well, fuck me," she grumbles.

Gladly, I think, and it surprises me how readily available that thought is.

A bit thrown by the subconscious admission that I would, indeed, love to see if Bluebell Allen has any other tattoos in illicit places, I smirk and try to project as much composure as I can.

"We have to stop meeting like this, Bonnie Bluebell."

Her gem-like eyes fly to mine, wide and sparkling until she realizes it's me. Then, they glass over, her expression turning chilly.

I guess my large tip didn't make much of a difference after all.

"Indy." Her dark-painted lips flatten into a straight line. She regards the boards on the floor again, sighs, and starts to pick them up and haphazardly place them back on the shelf.

"Here, let me help you," I say, coming around to her side of the aisle. Maybe a little helpful chivalry will do what the tip didn't.

"I don't need your help," she mutters. But she stumbles backward as she tries to lift an armful of two-by-fours. I reach out and catch her around the waist before she can join the rest of the boards on the floor. Her cropped shirt raises a little, and my palm meets her soft, warm skin just above her ripped jeans. In a woosh, my breath is expelled from my lungs.

Damn, I liked that a little too much.

Belle scrambles to her feet and jumps away from me as if my hand scalded her. Okay, then...

"What are you even doing here?" she exclaims breathlessly as she frantically tugs her shirt lower over the hem of her jeans.

"Nice to see you again, too." I chuckle. When she doesn't move or speak, I clear my throat. "Annie's house needs some work, so I figured I'd get started. What about you?"

Belle tugs on her shirt again, clearly self-conscious. "I need supplies for my Halloween display," she says simply.

Typical Ironwood Flats behavior. Always needing to go above and beyond for Halloween, making the decorations bigger and more ridiculous every year. And, if I remember correctly, Belle was always the biggest and most ridiculous of them all when it came to the holiday.

I bend over to pick up the remaining two-by-fours and replace them on the shelf. "Ahh. I'll, uh... leave you to it, then." If there's one thing I don't want anything to do with, it's Halloween decorations. Doing it for my niece and nephew is fine, but I don't want to even *know* what Belle has planned.

I cross over to my side of the aisle to get my cart of stuff and make my way quickly to the checkout. It might be my imagination, but I think I can feel those blue-violet eyes on me the whole time.

But I don't have enough caffeine in me to even think about that right now. I need coffee and to get started on Annie's front porch. Stat.

CHAPTER 4

BELLE

WORKING AT THE BROKEN Spur is a great job for me. The hours are manageable, and the people who come in and out keep me interested. Making drinks is really just a series of tasks that are easy to accomplish, so it doesn't take too much brain power. But the pay isn't always great, especially with big groups who don't tip, like those jackasses who were in there on Friday night. And there sure as shit aren't any benefits. So, I also work as the part-time librarian at Ironwood Elementary. I love it there. The kids are cute, and they love my seemingly never-ending list of fun facts about each story we read.

Which is how I find myself standing outside the school on Monday morning to help with the rush of kids, parents, and vehicles at drop-off when none other than Mike Page walks up flanked by his niece and nephew in the most perfect, most adorable scene known to woman.

I really need my ovaries to calm the fuck down. I can't be thinking of Mike as *perfect* or *adorable* just because he's doing the bare minimum by helping out his sister. Especially not after what happened in high school. I know that was a long time ago but seeing him again really brought up some shit. I could barely sleep on Friday night, and I hated myself for continually thinking about him. It was like my brain would not turn off. And then running into him at Lewis Hardware on Saturday morning, his perfect ass looking impossibly better in those sweatpants... it's enough to test anyone's resolve.

"Miss Allen!" Nicholas runs up to me. "I finished my book over the weekend. Do you have the next in the series?"

"I'm sure I do. Lyle brought it back last week, and I saved it for you. Stop by before recess, and you can check it out."

"Yes!" Nicholas pumps the air and jumps, his too-large backpack bouncing against his back. "Uncle Mike, are you picking us up after school, too?"

Mike gives Nicholas a fist-bump and says, "Sure, my man. If you want me to."

"I do!" Claire pipes up. She wraps her arms around Mike's waist and squeezes.

He rubs her back until she pulls away. "Okay, kiddo. I'll be here." He scrapes his palm against his chin as he watches them join their respective groups of friends and enter the school. His dark eyes slide my way, and I'm embarrassed to have been watching him that whole time. I try to avert my gaze, but I can't. He's just too good to look at.

I fully expect him to give me a cocky smirk, but he doesn't. He just smiles softly, the corners of his eyes crinkling. "He was in his room all weekend reading that book," he says. "I had to drag him outside to help me."

"Help you with what?" I ask.

"Fixing Annie's porch. And shutters." He shakes his head in dismay. "Jacob hasn't done much for a while, it would seem. But I wanted to teach Nicholas some of the handyman stuff my dad taught me, anyway, so it was a good opportunity."

My hands land on my hips. "Did you teach Claire, too?"

"Teach her what?" He looks genuinely confused.

I let out an exasperated puff of air. "The handyman stuff. Doesn't she deserve to know, too?" I sure wish someone had looked past the misogyny with which they were raised and taught me how to build or fix stuff around my house. As it stands, I'm building the set for the school's haunted house next week, and I've got ideas as big as Dallas and no skill to execute them.

Mike regards me for a moment, his gaze turning thoughtful. "You're right," he says after a while. "I should have had Claire out there, too. I will. Thanks for the reminder."

I open my mouth, ready to protest, until I realize he just said I was right. I close it with a snap. Now, I don't know what to do.

Luckily, he comes to my rescue. "How many witches did they hang in Salem?" he asks.

My brow furrows, and I rear back a bit at the change in topic. "What?"

"Your shirt." He points at it.

I look down. I had forgotten I was wearing my favorite Halloween shirt today. It says, *Salem Broom Company, established 1692.* "Oh. Nineteen." I straighten with pride at having yet another trivial fact at the ready.

"Nope." Mike grins.

"What do you mean, 'nope?'" I spit out. "I can name them all, too. Bridget Bishop, Sarah Good, Rebecca Nurse—"

Mike shakes his head, his grin widening. "Nope. Zero."

I narrow my eyes at him. "How are you going to tell me there were zero witches executed in Salem? It's basic history."

"None of them were witches," he says. "They were just people accused of witchcraft."

I bite the side of my cheek to keep myself from laughing. That was a pretty good one, if I'm being honest, but I can't let him know that. "You're insufferable," I say when I have my composure in check.

He purses his lips and nods. "I've been told that before." Shrugging, he lifts his arms away from his sides and lets them land with a slap. "Alas, I need to get back to it. Those porch steps aren't going to fix themselves."

I don't know what comes over me when he turns to walk away. Maybe it was that joke. Maybe it's his ass in those pants. But before I can think better of it, I call after him, "Hey!"

He turns around slowly. The outside is practically empty now; the other teachers have all made their way back inside behind the children to start their classes. As Mike regards me with a question in his dark eyes, I wish I hadn't stopped him. I should have let him walk away and out of my life like he did in high school. But the cat's out of the bag now, I guess.

"You think you could help me with a project? You know, since you're such a handyman?"

He takes a step closer to me and cocks his head. The wind hits just right to carry the scent of smoky cedar from his body. *Of course* the man smells amazing, too.

"What kind of project?" he asks.

"I have to build the set for the school's haunted house next week. That's why I was at the hardware store yesterday, but you saw how that turned out." I shrug as casually as I can. "I could use some help."

Mike chews on the inside of his lip, squinting up at the school in the mid-October sunlight. "For the kids?" he asks.

"Yeah. They do the trunk-or-treat outside, and then they come inside for the haunted house. My plan got a little... out of hand."

He chuckles, and the sound does something to my insides that I'm not proud of. "Typical Bonnie Belle," he says. "Always with the big ideas."

When we were in school, I would have taken that as an insult. I would have scoffed and made sure to body check his shoulder as I walked past. But there's no malice in it now. He almost sounds impressed.

"Sure. I can help." He flashes me a warm smile. Then, he raises his hand and rubs the back of his neck. "For the kids."

I let out a breath, relieved. "Right. Great. So, tomorrow?"

"Sounds good." He turns around to continue on his way, and I'm ashamed of how long I watch him go.

This was probably a big mistake. Spending time with Mike Page isn't high on my wishlist. But if it means this haunted house will get built, then so be it.

And if he wears those sweatpants again, I certainly won't complain.

CHAPTER 5

MIKE

"Okay." I clap my hands loudly as I stand in the doorway of Annie's bedroom. I can only see a lump under her comforter, but it moves at the sound. At least I know she's alive under there. "The house is clean. The porch steps won't kill you. The kids are at school for"—I check my watch—"two more hours. Time to get you out of bed." I sniff the air. "And into the shower."

"Fuck you," Annie's muffled voice sounds weak and quiet.

"Aww, you don't mean that," I croon.

"I very much do." She pulls the comforter tighter over her head. "Let me wallow in peace."

"No can do, Anna Banana." I'm pulling out all the stops with my childhood nickname for her. I use it in hopes that she'll at least pop her head out and glare at me, but she doesn't. She just remains still and silent.

Damn.

Time to change tactics. I fold my arms and lean against the doorframe. I'm going to be here for a while.

"I thought you said *you* kicked *him* out," I say.

"I did," she responds simply.

"This is not the behavior of a woman who has just liberated herself from the confines of a shitty relationship. We should be celebrating."

At that, she does pop her head out from under the comforter. Her hair is a bona fide rat's nest, and her eyes are bloodshot, but her expression is worth it. She's looking at me like I have three heads.

"What's with the feminist diatribe?" she croaks. Now that it's not muffled by the comforter, her voice sounds like she's been crying for weeks straight. Which she probably has.

Belle appears at the front of my mind, unbidden—her hands on her gloriously full hips as she took me to task for not teaching Claire how to use a hammer and saw like I taught Nicholas.

I shake my head to clear it. "It's hardly feminist. And hardly a diatribe." I mimic her thick, Texan drawl with each word.

She rolls her eyes. "I know you got that fancy degree and that fancy software engineer job up in Indiana," she intones, "but don't pretend you and I had different childhoods. You came from here, just like the rest of us."

I scoff. "So what? That means I can't be a modern man or join the twenty-first century?" Except, for all my talk, maybe I haven't if I left Claire out of the manual labor without even thinking. Sure, it's not *that* big of a deal, but for some reason, I want to impress Belle. Despite my upbringing, and despite what may have happened between Belle and me in the past, I want her to know I've changed.

This conversation has taken a turn I wasn't expecting, so before she can say anything else, I add, "Regardless, it doesn't take a feminist to know that you did the right thing kicking Jacob out on his ass. You can wallow, but you also have to shower."

She flops back on the bed and stares up at the ceiling. "But what am I going to do?" The last word is stretched and moaning, like the battery-operated ghost in the box of decorations I found in the shed. That thing scared the shit out of me.

"What do you mean, what are you going to do? You're going to participate in basic human hygiene. Maybe have dinner with your children who love you."

Annie slaps the comforter with both her hands on either side of her body. "That's not what I meant, you asshole. I mean about the rest of my life." Her voice cracks on the end like she's about to cry again. Sure enough, wetness glistens on her cheeks in the light between the curtains.

I let out a low whistle and sit on the edge of the bed, covering her hand with mine. "The rest of your life is kind of big, Anna Banana. Let's just start with the shower and a meal, huh? We'll figure the rest of it out as we go."

She sniffles and wipes her nose with the back of her hand. "Will you stay?" she asks, still staring up at the ceiling. Her voice is pitifully small and helpless. "Just for a few weeks?"

There's no way I'm leaving my baby sister in her time of need. I should be able to do most of my work tasks remotely, at least until Halloween. And while I miss my friends back in Indiana, they all have partners and flourishing careers now. I don't see as much of them as I used to.

And there's at least one person in Ironwood Flats that I wouldn't mind seeing more of.

"What's that look?" Annie asks, frowning up at me.

My eyes go wide. "What look?" I have no idea what my face was doing, but I was most definitely thinking about Belle again. If Annie caught it, it must have been obvious.

Annie bolts upright in bed, like a zombie coming back to life. "The one where you go all moon-eyed and smile like a doofus."

"I am not moon-eyed," I protest. "And I certainly do not smile like a doofus."

"Oh, yes you do." The finger she points in my face is topped with chipped nail polish. "Spill it."

"Don't change the subject. You need to shower, and you're not getting out of it."

She screws up her face in frustration. Now I'm in for it. Sure enough, she starts the interrogation. "You're the one changing the subject. Did you leave someone special behind in Indiana? Someone you haven't told me about?"

"No." The less information she gets, the better. She is very good at manipulating people into telling her what she wants to know. And I'd never lie to her, which she is also well aware of.

She narrows her eyes at me. "Michael Robert Page. You have been in town for all of seventy-two hours. Do not tell me you seduced some poor girl when you went out to that bar Friday night."

"The only people I saw at that bar were Old Man Peña and Bluebell Allen." And Annie's deadbeat soon-to-be-ex-husband, but she doesn't need to know that. Omitting information isn't *actually* lying.

Annie's eyes go even wider. "Did you fuck Belle Allen?"

"Dammit, Annie! No!"

She narrows her eyes and points her chipped nail polish at me again. "You better not. That girl was so pissed at you after you graduated."

"What? Why?" I know I wasn't the nicest to her when we were in school, but I don't think there was a singular thing I did that would have pissed her off more than she usually was at me.

But Annie rolls her eyes dramatically. "Oh, come on. Everyone heard the rumors." She looks at me expectantly, but when I just shake my head, she continues. "About how you made out with her behind the bleachers, and the next day you had moved on to Stacey-what's-her-name."

I screw up my face, trying to remember. "Stacey Villarreal?"

Annie snaps her fingers. "That's the one."

"Stacey and I never..." but I trail off. Like a bad penny, the memory comes right back up.

I had kissed Belle behind the bleachers. That, I remember clear as day. What's fuzzy is Stacey Villarreal. I never kissed her, but we did hang out after the thing with Belle.

I thought it was fine. Belle had told me she hadn't ever kissed anyone, and she was nervous to graduate without experiencing it. So, I told her I would do it. It was a good kiss. Great, even. But when it was over, she had said, "Thank you," and walked away. I figured she got what she came for, and that was that.

Which, in retrospect, only an idiot would think. But I was eighteen, about to graduate high school, and... well... an idiot.

"Belle told Maggie, who told Jackie, who told me," Annie is saying when I come to. "So even if that's not what happened, that's how she perceived it. You know Maggie and Jackie would never start unnecessary drama."

That is absolutely false, and that ridiculous chain of telephone proves it. But I also believe the drama queens in this instance. Even though I remember it differently, Belle's standoffishness on Friday night would suggest her wounds go deeper than a little harmless teasing. I even busted out my best jokes this morning to try to get her to laugh because her attitude threw me. I think I almost succeeded.

"I'm going to help her build the haunted house at the kids' school tomorrow," I say. I flash Annie my most charming grin. "I can win her over."

Annie groans. "Oh no. Please do not. The last thing that girl needs is to kiss you and watch you walk away again."

I shake my head as my grin falls. "I'm not talking about kissing her again." Okay, that's a teeny lie, but I still don't think it counts. "I'm talking about making amends. It's the right thing to do, don't you think?"

She eyes me skeptically. "That's not how this works."

"It'll be great. You'll see. Now"—I grab her arms and tug as I stand, pulling her out of the bed—"shower. You're stinking up the place."

CHAPTER 6

BELLE

"A little more to the left."

"I'm pretty sure this is exactly where it started," Mike grumbles as he stands on a ladder, hanging the last of my fabric ghosts on the tunnel we built. The idea is that everyone will enter this way, and they will both see and feel the ghosts in the tunnel. The strobe light and fog machine should give it an extra layer of creepiness. But not too creepy. This is for grade school kids, after all.

To be honest, though, I haven't been paying much attention to where the ghosts are being placed. Having Mike's ass practically at eye-level for the past hour has been distracting, to say the least.

The school library is closed for the rest of the week to set up for the haunted house. Or, rather, the haunted library. The rest of the school is functioning like normal, but the library has black paper taped over the interior and exterior windows so no one can see inside. Before Mike hung the paper, I put up signs that said:

NO BONES ABOUT IT. THIS WILL BE THE BEST HAUNTED HOUSE
EVER!

RAISING THE ROOF... AND MAYBE SOME SPIRITS!

FRIGHTENING RENO-VAMP-TIONS IN PROGRESS!

Mike had groaned at the last one, saying the pun didn't flow right. But when he thought I wasn't looking, he re-read it and chuckled, so I think he was just teasing me.

Once he hangs the last ghost, he hops of the ladder and puts his hands on his waist to study his handiwork. After a moment, he gives a nod of approval.

"What's next, boss?" he asks.

I rub my lips together and hum as I take in the space. As much as I want to keep him here, I know he's busy with Annie and her house. He's already been here for four hours. "I don't think I need you for anything else."

His dark eyes survey the room, then land on me. One corner of his mouth tips up in a soft smile. "I could come back tomorrow, if you need."

I'm pretty sure I smudge my lipstick by chewing on my bottom lip. His gaze dips to watch the motion, then back to meet mine, somehow darker than before. Just for a moment, though. It's gone as quickly as it came.

If I didn't know any better, I'd say Mike was thinking about my lips just then.

Do I want him to be thinking about my lips?

Honestly, this whole afternoon has been more fun than I anticipated. And not only because he wore his sweatpants and backwards hat again. He's turned into a nice guy over the years. Helpful. Funny. He teases me, but not out of malice. It's more like he is trying to goad me into playing around. After a while, I gave in and teased him back.

It was... nice.

"If you have time, I wouldn't mind help setting up the pumpkin scavenger hunt and the eyeballs. Oh, and the mystery doors." I say. I don't really need the help. It'll probably only take me one more afternoon to get it set up, but if he wants to come back, who am I to refuse him.

"I'm sorry, the what?" His brows are furrowed with concern. And if I didn't know any better, I'd say he looked a little green.

"The mystery doors?" I ask. "They're doors the kids open for a surprise—"

"No, no," he cuts me off, then swallows hard. "The eyeballs."

I watch him for a moment, sure he's fucking with me. But no, he seems genuinely nauseous.

Rolling my lips together can't contain my laughter, and a little snort escapes against my will. "They're just peeled grapes," I assure him. "I put them in a big bowl and hide them under a box with a little curtain. The kids reach their hands in to feel them."

"That's..." Mike trails off and shakes his head in dismay. "That's disgusting."

"It's Halloween!" I exclaim, stretching my arms out wide as if to remind him of what we've been doing here. "It's fun."

"No," he insists, almost as if he's talking to himself. "It is not." He shudders, then looks at me and straightens quickly, like he remembers I'm watching him. "The germs, I mean. That has to be a cesspool."

"Right," I say slowly. "You don't have to play cool with me, Indy. I knew you in high school back when we were all nerds, remember?"

He scoffs at that. "Speak for yourself. I was super popular, and everyone loved me."

He's kidding again. I know he is. But something about it reminds me that I wasn't cool enough for him to do more than poke fun at and kiss one time, and it hurts.

Not only was I not cool enough, I *asked him* to kiss me. And he did, but it must not have been anything spectacular because he moved on in less than twenty-four hours.

Shaking myself out of the memory, I start gathering the paint supplies that are strewn out on a drop cloth just for something to do with my hands. I can't believe how mortified I am about that, even over twenty years later. "I'm sure Annie is expecting you back. You can come tomorrow. Or not, if the eyeballs are too gross for you. I'm only judging you a little." The joke falls flat, and I mentally kick myself for being so awkward.

"Woah," Mike says, his voice raised slightly above the sound of me pounding the paint can closed. "What just happened here?"

I shrug, taking a handful of paint brushes and the paint can to the storage closet behind the circulation desk. "Nothing. Just trying to get cleaned up before I have to help with bus duty."

He stays planted on the other side of the desk. "I thought today was a day off that you were using to work on this."

"Might as well help as long as I'm here. I'll see you later, okay?"

I'm not looking at him, so I jump when his warm hand covers mine where it rests on the doorknob of the supply closet. His chest grazes my shoulder, and it sends tingles down my spine. His smoky cedar scent hits me at almost the same time. My breath feels like sandpaper in my lungs.

"Belle," he says. It might be the first time I've heard him call me that. At least, the first time since he's been home. And I like the sound of it way too much.

"Yeah?" I look up at him, lips parted. His gaze roams around my face, and we are so close that I can feel his breath tickling my skin.

"I'm sorry." His voice is deep and raspy, almost an octave deeper than usual.

"For what?" I all but whisper. I'm having a hard time catching my breath. From the rise and fall of his chest, he's feeling the same.

He huffs a laugh. "For whatever I said that made you panic-clean." His eyes bounce between mine as he adds, "And for being an ass in high school."

I shake my head and try to back away, but his grip on my hand tightens. When I meet his gaze again, it's the sincerest I've ever seen it.

"I was. That kiss—"

"Oh god," I groan. "We do not have to talk about that."

"We should," he insists gently. "It's possible I misread the situation, and I'm deeply sorry."

"There wasn't anything to misread," I say. "I don't know what I was thinking."

Yes, I do. I was thinking that I had never been kissed, and Mike's lips had been enticing me for years. Just like they have been for the past few days. But he doesn't need to know that.

"We were kids," he says. "I didn't know how to handle it."

"Neither of us did," I assure him, then I laugh. I can feel the heat rising in my cheeks. "I'm pretty sure I thanked you and ran away."

He chuckles, too, which goes a long way toward making me feel better. "You did. I thought you had enough, and that was that."

Swallowing hard, I shake my head slowly, my eyes never leaving his. "I think..." I trail off and take a deep breath, firming my resolve. Now that this can of worms has been opened, I might as well come clean. "I didn't know how to ask for more. And then the next day, when I saw you with Stacey..."

Mike rolls his eyes at himself. "I was such an idiot."

"No. Truly. You had no way of knowing." I bite my lip as I try to smile lightly. "Water under the bridge?"

He grins then, his pearly white teeth showing between his soft lips. "Yeah." He nods once and backs away from me. I immediately regret the lack of his hand on mine, so I shove it in my pocket.

"See you tomorrow?" I ask as he makes his way toward the door.

"It's a date," he says.

I'm just about to keep up my bold streak and ask him if that's a double entendre when he faces me and says, "I would have kissed you again, you know." And then he turns on his heel and walks out, leaving me to gape after him.

What the hell am I supposed to do with that?

CHAPTER 7

MIKE

WE FINISH SETTING UP the haunted library on Wednesday. The "eyes" are disgusting, but I manage to peel my share of the grapes with only a little gagging. Belle seems happy to have the extra help. At the end of our last day, she sighs contentedly and smiles at me. It simultaneously makes me feel like I've won the lottery and want to draw more of those happy sighs out of her in indecent ways.

I spend most of the day Thursday fixing up Annie's nail studio so she can see clients again and trying not to think about Belle's sparkling, blue-violet eyes and berry-red lips.

Nicholas decides he wants to be a dalmatian, and Claire has her heart set on being a butterfly, so I pick them up from school under the guise of taking them to the store for costume supplies. Really, I'm hoping to catch a glimpse of Belle, even though she said she isn't in the library on Thursdays.

Annie and I work on the kids' costumes late into the night. We toil mostly in silence, but it's nice to see her up and participating in life. She heads to bed before I do. On her way, she lays a hand on my shoulder and squeezes it affectionately. Her nail polish has been re-applied—orange and purple this time—and I smile softly at her self-care.

When my phone dings the next morning, I can barely move. I somehow managed to face-plant into the couch the night before, and when I crack an eye open, it looks like Halloween threw up on the floor of the living room. I had been too tired to clean up last night.

"Uncle Mike! Look at me!" Claire's high-pitched voice pierces through my early-morning haze. I squint both eyes open to see her in the butterfly costume, giant orange-and-black wings bobbing behind her as she bounces on her toes. I worked hard on the frames for those things, and seeing her love them fills my heart with joy.

Nicholas is also wearing his costume—complete with spots painted on his face—when he comes crawling into the living room. He woofs a few times, then pants and chomps his teeth as if to bite Claire's leg. She screams, and I wince.

"Too early for that," I groan as I push myself up to sitting. I'm still in my clothes from the night before, too. Who knew pseudo-parenting would be kind of like spending the night at a bar, except without the booze.

Annie's raspy laughter fills the room. I look over to see her hair done, clothes on, and face fully made up. I smile at that, too. My baby sister's back.

"Let's let Uncle Mike get back to his beauty sleep," she says. "Come on, kids. Time for school."

I scrub my face with my palm, trying to rub some life into it. "You're letting them wear their costumes to school?"

All three of them stare at me as if I grew a third eye. "It's Friday," Nicholas says as if that means something.

"And?" I ask.

"Next weekend is Halloween," Claire supplies unhelpfully.

"Okay…"

Annie finally comes to my rescue. "The school always does their Halloween parties the weekend before Halloween so everyone is free to go to the celebration downtown on actual Halloween." She leans in to mutter the next part, as if the kids can't hear her. "They hop the kids up on sugar before letting them run around at the trunk-or-treat and haunted house. It's a win-win."

"At the trunk-or-treat where they… get more sugar?" I narrow my eyes at her as if it should be obvious why this is a terrible idea.

She shrugs. "It's Halloween. Live a little."

My phone dings again from where I left it charging across the room. Annie shuffles the kids out the door, and it's suddenly, blissfully silent. I shove myself off the couch, my joints cracking like a Halloween glow stick, and pull my phone off the charger. My heart skips when I see two messages from Belle lighting up my screen.

> Belle: I need your help.

> Belle: Chase called in sick today. He has the flu. He was supposed to be the monster behind Mystery Door 2. Can you fill in?

I want to help Belle more than I hate the idea of participating in a haunted house. It's for kids, right? How bad could it be to dress up like a monster and shout boo when they open a door?

Eyeing the remnants of the Halloween costumes on the floor, I text back:

Mike: Sure thing. I can think of something.

The three dots dance at the bottom of the screen, then disappear, then reappear again before a message comes through.

Belle: You could just go as yourself. No costume necessary.

I throw my head back and cackle. Oh, it's on now. If she wants a monster, I'll give her a monster.

CHAPTER 8

BELLE

ALL I CAN DO is gape at Mike's costume. I blink a few times, hoping I'm not seeing what my brain says I'm seeing, but no luck. He's standing in front of me with his head poking out of the middle of a giant shirt that must be held up with some kind of wire frame. There's red blood at the top where a neck would be, and blood dripping down from where his actual head sits cradled in two fake arms. The face paint is what really does it, though. He's got white paint slathered over his skin, and dark circles under his eyes that are so realistic, it looks like he's truly undead.

Annie must have been in on this. There's no other explanation for a makeup job that good.

"You are going to terrify the children," I say flatly.

He scoffs. "Isn't that the point?"

"No," I all but laugh. This has to be the most ridiculous thing I've ever seen. "The point is to have fun. And, I repeat, they're *children*."

He shrugs, which has the disconcerting effect of bobbing the entire costume up around his head and back down. "You said monster. I delivered." He looks me up and down. "It's better than your costume."

"I'm a witch!" I exclaim, as if it weren't obvious. I've got the hat, the black hair, the dark lipstick and nail polish, and I even put fishnet tights under my ripped jeans.

Mike tilts his head, which is so gross, I have to look away. "You barely look any different than normal," he says. It's not unkind. Just a statement of fact. And he's not wrong, but that's what kid-friendly costumes are about—a hint at something else. Not this hyper-realistic terror-fest I'm looking at in front of me.

"You're the man who squirmed through peeling grapes because I called them eyeballs," I say incredulously. "How are you possibly wearing *this* right now?"

"It's different when I'm the one scaring. Honestly, I get it now. This is going to be amazing." He rocks back and forth on his heels, which is so creepy, it makes me gag.

But then something occurs to me. "Wait a minute, do you hate Halloween because you're... scared?"

His eyes widen, and that's when I know I've caught him. There has always been something off about how he reacts to the Halloween shenanigans of this town. I thought he simply hated it here, but it's all adding up now. Mike Page is a scaredy-cat.

"Oh my god. You are." I cover my mouth with my hands as if that can keep the laughter inside.

"Everyone's obsession with skeletons and zombies and... death. And pumpkins! It's weird." He tries to justify it, but the fake shoulders of his costume are shaking, too. "I hear it," he says. "I know how stupid that sounds."

"No, not at all," I pat his costume arm. "Everyone has something they're irrationally afraid of."

He cocks a... hip? Except with the weird placement of the costume, it looks like his thigh is out of place. "Oh yeah? What's yours?"

"Bugs," I say without hesitation.

He leans forward as if he didn't hear me right. "Bugs?"

I open my arms wide and turn in a slow circle. "Do you see any spiders in here?"

"Well... no," he admits.

"That is by design. Can't deal with them. Never could."

He turns the corners of his lips down and nods slowly as if in respect. I don't think I'll ever get used to seeing his detached head move in any way.

"Belle! We're opening the doors. The kids are coming!" one of the first grade teachers says from the front of the library. I eye Mike up and down again. Nothing to do now but let him scare the shit out of the children. Holding open Mystery Door number two, I usher him inside. He waggles his eyebrows at me before I shut the door, and I can't help but giggle at how weird it looks. I narrow my eyes at the door for a minute, thinking, then scrawl out a sign that reads: BEWARE! OPEN AT YOUR OWN RISK! and tape it on just before the kids descend into the library.

There's a lot of ohh-ing and tittering as they make their way through the strobe-lit, ghost-ridden entryway. Once each child emerges into the transformed library, the volunteer teachers and I hand them a pumpkin scavenger hunt sheet. The goal is for them to find all twelve pumpkins, and everyone who does wins a prize. As they look, the kids stop by the apple-bobbing station. They squeal with delight at the eyeball bowl. The battery-operated talking skeleton is a huge hit. And Mystery Doors one and three get opened several times.

Just when I'm considering taking the sign on Mike's door down, a butterfly stands tall in front of it. I casually walk over so I can run interference if I need. From the profile, I can see the butterfly is, in fact, Claire, and I wonder if she knows what her uncle is wearing.

She puts a steady hand on the doorknob, then pulls it open slowly. Mike is standing inside, casually waiting. When the door is fully open and Claire can see his whole costume, he smiles, his teeth almost glowing in the blacklights we hung in this area on Tuesday.

"Hi," he says simply.

That's enough to make Claire scream at the top of her lungs. But right before I jump in to save her, she doubles over and holds her belly, cackling. She laughs so hard that she falls to the ground and literally rolls.

"Do it again!" she cries, jumping up to shut the door in Mike's face. She runs across the room, grabs two of her friends, then waves Nicholas over, too. They all line up in front of the door, then one of the little girls opens it.

This time, Mike sways back and forth a little before he pops his eyes open and winks. The kids all devolve into hysterical laughter. It's music to my ears.

A small crowd gathers, and before they shut the door again, he catches my gaze. His wild, scary smile softens, and his decapitated head nods at me. I shake my own, but the grin is permanently stuck to my face for the rest of the night.

After a few hours, parents make their way inside to drag their tired, protesting children home. I don't envy their job of trying to calm down kids wired with too much candy and fun. When I open Mike's door to tell him the night is over, he looks so happy. It melts my heart.

"Time to clean up?" he asks. Shit, it's really nice he offers to do that, too.

"No," I say. "We leave most everything up through Halloween. The eyeballs get thrown away, obviously"—I pull a face, and he laughs—"and the mystery doors will have book displays behind them, but everything else can stay."

"Oh." He sounds disappointed as he comes out from behind the door. "Cool."

The way he lingers would suggest that he's not ready for the night to be over yet. And, truly, neither am I. I've been looking forward to these interactions with him. When Chase called in sick, I could have asked eight other people to come help, but I texted Mike first. I wanted to see him tonight. That has to mean something.

I clear my throat and straighten my spine. "Some of the teachers do a post-party bonfire down by the river. Do you maybe want to go?" And then I add, "If you take that gruesome-as-fuck costume off. I'm not going anywhere with you looking like that."

The smile on his face grows impossibly wider. "I'd love to."

CHAPTER 9

MIKE

"WHAT IS THIS?" I lift a brown bottle out of the cardboard carrier at my feet. Belle offered to grab some beer before she picked me up, but this bottle has a giant jack-o'-lantern on the side.

"It's a pumpkin beer from a brewery in Austin." She doesn't take her eyes off the dark stretch of road in front of us.

I look at her incredulously. "You drink this?"

"It's local," she says by way of explanation.

"It's *pumpkin*," I counter.

Her blue-violet eyes flick my direction, then back to the road. "Are you surprised because it's sweet, or because it represents a holiday you despise?"

"I don't hate Halloween, per se," I say, reeling back in my seat, but even I can hear it's unconvincing.

She barks out a harsh laugh. "Who are you trying to fool, me or yourself?"

There's no time to answer her, though, because we pull up next to a handful of cars in a little alcove near the river. She pointedly plucks the beer off my lap and gets out of the car, and I scramble to follow.

Off in the distance, there is a small bonfire already raging. About fifteen people in varying states of costume are scattered around. A few sit by the water, looking out at it. Some are laughing by the fire. Others seem to be strolling along a path away from where we're parked. Belle saunters up to the group, waving and chatting with people as she passes. You'd think with it being such a small town that I'd recognize at least one or two of the people here, but they mostly seem to be transplants from surrounding towns, or they married someone whose name I do recognize but don't see here.

In fact, it doesn't seem like anyone brought a guest from outside the school. I don't know if that's supposed to make me feel weird or special.

There are two large, blue coolers sitting a little ways away from the fire. Belle unloads her beer into one, saving a bottle for herself. She takes out another and wiggles it in my direction.

"When in Rome?" she asks playfully.

I shrug. "Sure."

She uses an opener on her keychain to pop off the tops. I take one from her and sip from it, letting the liquid swish around in my mouth a little.

"Hmm," I hum thoughtfully. "It's more spiced than sweet. Very fall."

Her eyebrows tick up as she smirks. "I'm a bartender. You really think I'd steer you wrong?"

I search her eyes, on fire with twin reflections of the flickering flames. "No," I say finally. That one word feels weighted with meaning, though I'm not entirely sure what I'm trying to convey. Annie was right when she said I do not need to sleep with Bluebell Allen and then go back to Indiana. It would be wrong to lead her on like that. Again, apparently, if that kiss in high school meant to her what I think it did.

But the way her eyes have caught mine right now has me bewitched. I can't imagine breaking the spell.

The night is warm, and with the fire at my back and the heat passing between us, I'm starting to regret my choice of jeans, t-shirt, and open flannel shirt. I'm about ready to shrug out of the flannel when Belle sips her beer and says, "Want to take a walk?"

I peer at the people milling around the flames. "You don't want to hang around with your friends?"

She tips her head back and forth while pursing her lips. "I see them every day." Her gaze shifts to somewhere in the distance behind me. "I'd rather talk to you."

It feels like an admission she wasn't quite sure about giving, and I'm strangely honored that she'd want to spend any time with me at all. I turn my body to the side and motion in the direction she had been looking. "Lead the way," I tell her.

We walk slowly away from the growing crowd of people, drinking in silence. It gets much cooler away from the flames, but I can still feel the heat of Belle's body as we veer closer to each other on the uneven path.

She kicks at some rocks with her combat boots. "So," she starts awkwardly. "Why do you hate Halloween?"

I huff a laugh. "Why do you love it so much?" I deflect.

"Mmm-mmm." She shakes her head. "You first."

Sighing, I drop my shoulders into a defeated slump. "When I was young, my sisters used to gang up on me. They'd hide skeletons in closets and noise-making ghosts in trees. Stupid pranks." I laugh lightly at the memory. "But I was young, you know? I lived in terror in the weeks leading up to it, and I was always so glad when it was over."

Belle is silent for a long while. I look over at her, and she's staring in the opposite direction, out at the water. Her shoulders are shaking ever so slightly.

"You're laughing at me!" I say, surprised.

"I'm not!" she insists, though her voice is shaky with repressed giggles.

"You know what? Fine. No more information for you."

She playfully shoves my shoulder. "I just can't imagine Mike Page as a scared little kid, okay? It's cute."

I should be insulted. But hearing Belle call me cute—even in this context—makes my heart swell. We stop and hold each other's gazes in the dark. For a moment, I consider pulling her to me and kissing her, but then she speaks, and it's gone.

"Fair's fair," she says as we continue walking. "I like Halloween because..." She trails off and runs a hand up and down as if showing me her clothing. It's the exact same outfit she was wearing for the haunted house, just without the witch hat. "This is me. Surely, you remember from high school that this is how I've always been. During this season, everyone seems to bring out their spooky side a little, and I feel like I fit in."

My chest suddenly feels tight. She's dressed like this for as long as I can remember. She must have always felt this way, and I certainly didn't do anything to help make that any better.

"I'm sorry I teased you about it so much in high school," I almost whisper.

Her pointed gaze lands sidelong on me. "Water under the bridge, remember?"

I nod, and we walk slowly in silence. She finishes the last of her beer and tosses both our empty bottles in a garbage can that lines the path before coming back next to me.

"Why did you leave?" she asks.

"Why didn't you?" I return. "This place can be stifling. You said yourself you never felt like you fit in. Why stay in a place that makes you feel like that?"

"I didn't know what to do after high school. Eventually, I guess I found my groove." She toes some dirt on the path. "You're right, it can feel stifling here, but it's also beautiful."

We pause for a moment outside of a wooded area, looking out at the crescent moon reflected on the river. There are more stars out here than in Indiana, that's for sure. But the most beautiful thing in this scene is her.

"Why did you ask me to kiss you?" My voice is hoarse with desire.

She turns to face me, her eyes wide and lips parted. I can almost make out the flush of her cheeks in the moonlight. The need to take her right now surges in me, and I have to clench my hands to make them stay where they are.

"Because I wanted to kiss you," she says simply. And then, because it's her turn to ask a question, she says, "Will you do it again?"

My breath is expelled from me in a quick woosh. "Fuck yes." My arms circle her waist as I bring her body flush against mine. Her fingers waste no time threading themselves through my hair. And in a split second, our lips meet.

She tastes like pumpkin spice and hops, and her lips are even softer than I remember. I tease at the seam of them with my tongue, and she opens readily for me. Her nails scrape at my scalp as she tries to pull me closer. Needing me. Devouring me.

But I need her, too, in a way I've never needed anyone else. It's like she's been here, waiting for me all along, and I just had to look around and see it.

We break apart, breathless, and while I'm desperate to feel more of her body pressed up against mine, I don't want to do anything she might think is a mistake. I like her. Even though I'm leaving soon, I don't want another twenty years of pent-up miscommunication between us. That's not fair to her.

"That was way better than it was in high school," she breathes.

"Are you saying I was a bad kisser?"

Her laugh is an airy thing, and I want to bottle it up like a potion. "Not at all. But it seems like we've both learned a thing or two."

"I've learned lots of things," I say darkly. Apparently, that kiss has addled my brain, because there's no way I would have said that if I were thinking clearly.

The smirk that plays at her lips lets me know I haven't crossed a line yet. "Oh yeah?" she asks coyly. Her chin juts out in the direction of the trees behind us. "Show me?"

There is nothing in the world I want to do more than to drag those jeans and fishnets down over her ass and bury myself in her soft center, but Annie's voice in my head is feebly trying to warn me away.

"I'm leaving in a week," I croak out. "I can't stay."

"I know." She reaches out and lifts the hem of my shirt to drag a black-painted fingernail against the skin just above my jeans. "It can just be fun." Her dark eyebrows tick up suggestively.

All my reservations are thrown out the window with the glittering playfulness in her eyes. We've both matured since we were in high school. She's right. It can just be fun. We don't have to make it weird. And there's nothing I want more than to explore every part of her.

I grab her hand, and she laughs deeply as we run for the trees.

CHAPTER 10

BELLE

THE MINUTE WE'RE BEHIND the tree line, our hands are on each other again. I slide mine underneath his shirt as our lips meet, and he shivers.

"Cold?" I ask breathlessly.

"No," he rasps. His palms find my ass, and he grips it to lift me as he takes two steps forward to press my back into the trunk of a tree. I wrap my legs around his torso, using the tree as leverage to keep some of my weight off him. He groans and presses his lips to mine again. We're all frantic lips and tongues and teeth, hands clutching at clothes and skin as we try to make as much contact as possible. We devour each other as if we don't have much time. Which, I suppose, is true. Technically, anyone could come back this way at any time, though we're far removed from the rest of the people here.

Mike slides one of my legs off of his hip and down to the ground. The other, he grips under my thigh and angles it so his hard length presses against my center. I roll my hips into his, chasing as much friction as I can get. There are too many layers between us, but I'm not sure what's on the table. I didn't exactly have a plan when I suggested we could have some fun. I only had a wild desire for more of him.

His fingers work their way under my sweater to graze the underside of my breasts while his lips continue to bruise mine. He swallows my moan, then works his fingers under my bra to tease my nipple. The sensation sends me out of my body. That's the only explanation for why I start grinding against him like a horny teenager. But he seems into it, because he breathlessly pulses his hips to meet mine.

"More," I sigh. "I want more, Mike. Please."

He pulls away, his hooded eyes dark with need. It's hard to make out all of his features, but the moonlight filtering through the tree branches dapples his face in a silvery glow. *Perfection*, is all I can think as I study the way his cheekbones stand out in sharp relief. The way his jaw ticks as he considers my request. The way his hair is mussed, and his lips are stained. I did that, I realize dimly, and that awareness sends a new wave of yearning straight through me.

Suddenly, he steps back, dropping my other leg to the ground. He wordlessly spins me around so I'm facing the tree, reaches around my waist, and undoes the fly of my jeans. Wasting no time, he shimmies his hand under the waistband of my fishnets and panties. His finger strokes my clit as he keeps me upright with his other arm around my waist.

"Fuck, Belle," he moans into the fabric of my sweater. "You're so wet. Spread your legs a little more so I can feel you."

I do as I'm told and am rewarded with both Mike's satisfied hum and his finger teasing my entrance. He angles his hand so he can dip it inside me as he reaches his other hand back under my sweater to tease my nipples. My hips rock back and forth, trying to urge his finger deeper inside.

"Do you like that, baby?" he asks quietly.

"Yes," I hiss. "But..." I trail off, not sure how to ask for what I want. Instead of saying it, I reach down and slide my jeans down my hips to give him better access. Mike practically growls and uses the hand that's not inside me to pull down my fishnets and panties. It's still warm in the Texas autumn, but the fresh air on my skin sends shivers up and down my spine.

Mike alternates between circling my clit and fucking me with his finger until I'm panting and squirming. He grinds his hips against my ass, and I'm suddenly desperate for more. I reach behind myself to undo the fly of his jeans. When my hand finally makes contact with his cock, he lets out an almost-feral sound.

"I want to fuck you against this tree. Can I?" He leans in to lightly bite my earlobe.

"Do you have a condom?" I tug on his cock again, and his breath comes more rapidly.

"Yes," he says simply, as if forming full sentences is too much to ask with his finger inside me and my hand wrapped around him. He untangles himself from me, and I look over my shoulder to see him taking a foil-wrapped package out of his wallet. He makes quick work of opening it and sliding it on.

"Bend over and put your hands on the tree trunk, Belle," he commands.

I am helpless to do anything but exactly what he says. The trunk of the tree is rough under my palms. Mike slides his hands up my inner thighs, coaxing them open further.

"Your ass is fucking perfect." His voice sounds almost reverent, as he grips the skin hard, spreading me open for him. He guides the tip of his cock over my clit, and I tremble with anticipation.

"You want this?" he asks as he glides the head through my wetness. "You want me to fuck you out in the open like this?"

"I want it, Mike. Please," I whimper. "I *need* it."

Before I can beg any more, he's inside of me. He stretches me deliciously full, both his hands on my ass now to help angle me for him. Slowly, he moves in and out, pushing further each time until he's fully seated.

"You feel incredible," he says. "Are you okay?"

"God yes," I breathe. "I haven't been this okay in a long time. Don't stop."

He chuckles as he slowly drags in and out, in and out. "All right then. But you have to be quiet for me. Can you do that?"

"I make no promises," I tease.

For that, I'm rewarded with a hard thrust. Our skin smacks together, and my palms scrape against the bark of the tree trunk. An "oh" escapes me, louder than I intended.

"Mmm-mmm," he cautions as he thrusts hard again. "I said you need to be quiet. You wouldn't want your friends knowing I'm fucking you over here, would you?"

"No," I groan as quietly as I can.

"Good girl," he whispers, reaching his hand around to play with my clit again. Before long, I'm shuddering and panting. Pressure starts to build at the base of my spine. I use the tree trunk for purchase as I meet his hips with my own. Little moans and breaths escape both of us as we work each other higher and higher. When he lifts my sweater over my breasts so he can grip them roughly with his palm, I let out a low sound that starts in my chest and works its way out into the night air.

"Shh," he cautions me.

"I'm so close," I whisper. "It feels so good."

The hand cupping my breast closes over my mouth. "Let go, baby," he says into the shell of my ear. "Come for me."

With a few more thrusts, I come undone. My body shakes in waves of pleasure. I cry out into Mike's hand, which muffles the sound. It isn't long before he follows me over the edge.

When our breathing slows enough, he pulls out. I quickly adjust my pants, and he removes the condom to do the same. He jogs back to the trash can on the path to dispose of it and is back at my side in a second. When he nears, he wastes no time gripping the back of my head and pulling me in for a slow, languid kiss. That kiss is everything—sensual and full of feeling. And even though my knees are weak and my mind is buzzing, I still want more. I want to see Mike naked in my bed. I want to ravage his body and wake up next to him.

"Come home with me."

It's a statement, not a question, but he doesn't hesitate. He smiles that pearly white grin and says, "Let's go."

CHAPTER 11

MIKE

BELLE AND I DON'T get much sleep. The way her body fits with mine is intoxicating. It seems she feels the same way, because we can barely keep our hands off each other the whole night. When her eyelids finally start drooping at around two in the morning, I kiss her forehead and tell her to sleep. She's out in seconds.

I doze a little, but my mind is racing. Every nerve ending is on fire. Belle—naked and laying on her stomach next to me with her upper back exposed over her comforter—is so fucking gorgeous. I don't want to close my eyes and sleep. My time here is short; I don't want to waste another minute not looking at her.

Eventually, the birds start chirping outside. There's no light coming in through her bedroom window yet, but I'm restless. I don't want to wake her—especially because I know she's got a late shift at The Broken Spur tonight—so I get out of bed as carefully as I can, pull on my boxers, and walk to her kitchen.

I put my hands on my hips and look around. We went straight to the bedroom last night, so I didn't have much time to explore. But when I see an espresso machine and milk steamer in the corner of her counter, I know I've hit the jackpot. If there's one thing I know how to do, it's make lattes.

It only takes a few minutes to find everything I need. Her espresso machine looks brand new—not a stain or a scuff to be found. It makes me think she's never used it before.

Somehow, it's unsurprising to find a set of mismatched mugs in her cabinet. A few are chipped, and one is missing a handle. I take down the two biggest ones I can find and get to work brewing the espresso and steaming the milk.

My phone buzzes on the counter where I left it last night. I'm surprised the thing still has a charge. When I pick it up to look at it, I wish it were dead. Instead, rapid-fire messages from all four of my sisters light up the screen.

> Annie: Guess who didn't come home last night.

> Lindsey: Your deadbeat husband?

> Annie: Bitch. I kicked him out weeks ago. Mikey has been with me helping out.

> Lisa: Glad to see you didn't let him crawl back again.

> Erica: Leave Annie alone. We're proud of you, Anna Banana.

Annie: You're missing the point. Mikey didn't come back from his date last night.

Lisa: Mikey had a date???

Annie: Yup. With that Allen girl.

Lisa: Belle???

Lindsey: She's still in the Flats? I thought for sure she'd get out by now.

Annie: It's not so bad here. Which you would know if you ever came back to visit.

Leave it to Annie to kill the group chat with a guilt trip. It finally goes quiet, and for a minute, I dare to hope that might be the end of it.

No such luck.

Annie: Mikey, are you alive or what?

Erica: We can see he's read the messages.

Annie: All the more reason to demand a response. He knows what he's done. He's leaving that poor girl in a week, and she's had a thing for him since high school.

And that's about where I have to chime in.

Mike: She has not had a thing for me since high school. We kissed once.

Lisa: You did???

Lindsey: How did we not know.

Erica: You had both left for college. From what I heard, it wasn't that big of a deal.

Annie: Agree to disagree.

Mike: In case you need a reminder, I'm forty years old. So is she. We are consenting adults. And that is all I am willing to say on the matter.

Again, there's a pause, and I think that must have actually worked. Maybe they respect my adult decision-making.

Erica: You're forty-one…

I grumble and shut my phone off. That's enough of that.

"A girl could get used to you hanging out in my kitchen in your boxers, making me lattes." Belle's voice comes from behind me, low and husky from just waking up. I turn around to see her in my flannel shirt from last night and not much else. The hem of it barely covers the curve of her ass, and I grow hard just looking at her gorgeous, bare thighs. I can't help but remember how they were wrapped around my hips last night.

I hand her one of the mugs, letting my fingers linger on hers. "A guy could get used to being here and making you lattes." It's out of my mouth before I can think about it. We stare at each other for a minute, both with our hands still on the mug, because we both know we can't get used to it. I'm leaving at the end of the week.

She takes the latte from me and sips it. Her eyes roll back in her head, and she moans. "Oh my god. This is so good. When the hell did you learn to make coffee like this? I haven't used that machine once yet because I can't figure it out."

"My buddy's family owns a coffee shop up in Indiana. Well, it's his now. I worked there off and on over the years."

It's as if the mention of Indiana douses cold water on us. Belle lowers her eyes, then sits at the kitchen table, cupping her hands around her mug. I take my own latte and sit next to her, close enough to smell her spiced shampoo, but far enough away that we're not touching.

She doesn't take her eyes off her mug. "This is... complicated."

"Yeah." I nod, swallowing hard. "I like you, Bonnie Bluebell."

Her gaze slides to mine, and she smiles sadly. "I like you too, Indy."

"That's not enough, is it?" I ask, knowing full well that the answer is no.

Blue-violet eyes sparkling, she shakes her head slowly. "It was fun though."

The suggestion that we could continue just having fun for the rest of the week is on the tip of my tongue, but even I know that's not a good idea. She's trying to let me down easy, and I should let her.

"It was," I say instead. We hold each other's eye contact, and I study her features as if committing them to memory. If I thought she was gorgeous before, she's absolutely breathtaking now. In the early morning light, stripped of her makeup, she's stunning. Those curves filling out my shirt should be illegal.

She's funny, beautiful, and we had the hottest sex I've ever had in my life last night among the trees.

Two realizations hit me like a ton of bricks. The first is that the only thing I want in the world is to stay here with her. The second is that if I don't leave right now, I'm never going to.

I slap my thighs and stand slowly. "I should probably get going. Annie has a few more things for me to do in her nail studio before she can start seeing clients again."

"Oh." Belle sounds surprised, but she shakes her head quickly as if to dislodge whatever thoughts were sticking there before she stands, too. "Right. Let me change so you can have your shirt back."

"Keep it." I let myself trail a finger down her jawline and soak up the softness of her skin one more time. "It looks better on you, anyway."

Because I can't help it, I press my lips to hers. It's a sweet kiss, if not a little sad. I pull away too soon and silently go back to the bedroom to find my t-shirt and jeans.

Once dressed, I come back out to the kitchen, where Belle is gazing out the window and still clutching her mug. She looks at me blankly when I throw back the dregs of my coffee and set the mug in her sink.

"Do you want a ride back to Annie's?" she asks.

As much as I want to spend more time with her, I know that wouldn't be a good idea. I shake my head. "It's only a little over a mile. I think I'll walk, if that's okay?"

She puts on the best smile she can. "Sure. See you around, Mike."

And then, without any room to second-guess myself, I leave out her front door and start walking home. But the whole way there, I can't get Belle out of my head.

If this is for the best, then why does it feel so wrong?

CHAPTER 12

BELLE

HALLOWEEN IN IRONWOOD FLATS is a big deal. Every year, after the school finishes their celebrations, practically the entire population gathers downtown to start setting the stage for the next weekend's festivities. It's never been an official thing. There are no social media invitations or even word-of-mouth. The Sunday before Halloween, we all just know to gather in the town square at ten in the morning and await instructions. The downtown businesses all participate in window-decorating contests, so some of us help the owners. The kids will trick-or-treat at each storefront next weekend, so some organize candy and small prizes. And the town square itself is transformed into a Halloween spook fest, complete with flying witches and ghosts hanging from the branches of trees, animatronic skeletons popping out from unexpected places, streamers, orange fairy lights, and giant blow-up yard decorations.

Years ago, it used to be that the townspeople would gather just before ten, the clock in the town square would chime, and everyone would randomly group together and find something to do. Now, it's a whole event in and of itself, with a greeting from the mayor, food tents from the downtown restaurants, and pumpkin everything. Coffee, pastries, pies—you name it. If someone has figured out how to put pumpkin in it, it's available for purchase. There are, of course, apple cider items, too. But everyone knows that the real star of the show is the pumpkin.

So, when I wake up Sunday after a long shift at The Broken Spur last night and without Mike in my bed this morning, I'm at least grateful I'll have something to do to take my mind off his absence.

I get dressed quickly and walk the short distance to the town square. The café is open, so I grab a pumpkin latte and a slice of pumpkin bread before making my way toward the center of town. People are milling around the fountain and chatting. A few of the elementary school teachers give me curious side eyes, and I'm sure I'll have some explaining to do on Monday for my hasty disappearance from the bonfire.

Tipping my head back and forth, I try to release some of the tension that's crept into my neck and shoulders over the past twenty-four hours. This feeling that has been plaguing me since Mike left my house is unpleasant, to say the least. I think I might miss him. Or, at least, I miss the way his body fit with mine. How his hands felt on my skin. The way his smoked cedar scent lingered in my hair long after he had gone.

I finish my pumpkin bread and move on to my latte. Unfortunately, when I take a sip, I cringe. It's fine, but it's not nearly as good as Mike's was.

Dammit. That man has ruined lattes for me now, too.

Grumbling internally, I take a look at where people are starting to congregate. There seems to be the fewest people outside the toy store, so I head over there. But I stop in my tracks when someone suddenly comes up beside me and loops their arm through mine. I catch a glimpse of bottle-blonde hair piled high on a woman's head, and then my grumble turns into an external one.

"Going to the toy shop?" Annie's voice is overly cheerful. "Me too. What a coincidence."

Nothing Annie Page has done in her entire life has ever been a coincidence. I believe that shit about as far as I can throw her. She saw me walking this way and inserted herself so she could get some gossip.

"Mike's not with you?" I ask as casually as I can.

I'm sure she sees right through that, but she flashes her gorgeous smile with those perfectly white teeth. "No. He took the kids mini golfing so I could have the day to myself. Isn't that just the sweetest?"

Fuck. It is the sweetest. As if I needed another reason to pine over him.

"And you decided to spend your morning here?" I'm shamelessly trying to figure out how far her scheming has gone. I wouldn't put it past her to have sent Mike to mini golf with the kids so she could come here and hope to chat with me.

She tilts her head and looks up at me. At just over five feet, Annie is tiny, but she is also fierce. The look she pins me with has me tensing as if I've done something wrong. "Where else would I be?" she asks. "As a proud Ironwood Flats resident, I take pleasure in helping the local businesses of this town prepare for the biggest shopping day of the year."

I tick up an eyebrow at her and silently wait for more. She laid that on a little too thick, so my guess is that mini golf was not Mike's idea. Though I wouldn't be surprised if he thought it was by the time she'd finished with him.

Annie sighs and rolls her eyes. "Ugh, fine. I came here hoping to see you." She stops us in the middle of the empty street and turns to face me, taking my hands in hers. Her manicure is perfect, which is a good sign that she's emotionally better off than she had been.

And a reminder that Mike did what he came here to do. His job is almost done.

"Are you okay?" She leans in conspiratorially and lowers her voice. "I love my brother, but I know how he is. He's not a love-'em-and-leave-'em kind of guy, exactly. But he doesn't stick around for long, either. When he didn't come home on Friday night, the only thing I could think was, 'Oh, that poor girl.'"

The mock-sympathy is a little much, but I think the sentiment is genuine. Annie is fiercely loyal to her family, but she's honest, too, and she doesn't like when they fuck up. In a small town like this, I can't really blame her. When someone makes a mistake, everyone knows about it. People have grown more empathetic over the years, but it's still considered a mark against your family name.

"Mike was a perfect gentleman," I reassure her. Well, sort of. I try to force my face not to redden as I remember the things he said to me in the woods. "We know what we're doing."

"I hope that's true." She tilts her head to the side, inquisitive.

There's no way I'm giving her more than that. If Mike hasn't spelled it out for her, it's not my place. "He's a really nice guy, Annie," I say simply.

Her eyes widen in surprise. "Ohmygod." She breathes it all as one word and leans in so close that I can smell the hairspray coming off of her head. "You *like* him."

"What?" I exclaim, jumping back. "No. I mean... he's starting to grow on me. In a totally platonic way. Nothing more than that. And, you know, the one night..." My cheeks are actually on fire now, and I force myself to stop rambling before I say something I'll truly regret.

"You do," she sings. "That's okay. Between you and me, I think he likes you, too."

"In a totally platonic—"

"Oh, will you shut up?" she cuts me off. "You two like each other. What's the big deal?"

"What's the big deal?" I repeat incredulously. "He's leaving at the end of the week!"

Annie shrugs as if this is inconsequential. "So what? You're both adults, as you said. Figure it out."

I gape at her, my jaw practically on the ground. I don't even have words for all the ways that's not possible.

She scoffs at my silence. "You mean to tell me that you two are just going to ignore the fact that you finally found someone you want to spend more time with, only to let it go because he lives in another state?" She shakes her head and raises her eyebrows. "That's the stupidest thing I've ever heard."

"Annie," I say, trying to be reasonable. "We don't just live in different states. We have *lives*. Jobs. Friends. One of us can't pick up and move because of a crush."

"You act like air travel isn't a thing. This isn't the 1930s, no matter how much this town might feel stuck there. Hang out. Switch off weekends. See if it's worth pursuing. I don't know; I can't solve this for you. But take it from me." She grows somber, then. "If you find someone you like, you should explore it. Don't settle for someone else."

With that, she turns on her heel to walk back toward the dry goods store, leaving my jaw dropped for the second time in less than thirty minutes. By the time I collect myself enough to remember what I was doing and where I was going, I realize Annie is walking in the opposite direction.

"Hey!" I call. "I thought you were going to help at the toy store."

She turns around, walking backwards as she talks. "Did I say that? Oh, I must have been confused. I'm helping at the dry goods store with Maggie and Jackie. You know how easy it is to get those two stores confused. But I'll see you soon!" She wiggles her fingers in a wave and turns around to all but sprint to the other side of the square.

I blink a few times to clear my head before joining the small group outside the toy store. We work until well into the afternoon to get everything perfect, but the whole time, I can't get what Annie said out of my brain. Even if it were possible to fly out to see each other frequently, would he even want to? Do I?

Ultimately, I make my way home with more questions than answers. And every time I think about calling Mike to see if there's any possibility that he might want to give this thing between us a shot, I remember how resolved he looked on Saturday morning when he left.

It leads me to believe that, no matter how much I might want this, he might not. And I don't think I can take that kind of rejection again. Even if I do fall asleep and dream of him smiling at me like I'm the best thing he's seen in a long time.

CHAPTER 13

MIKE

I DON'T HAVE ANY kids of my own, but my three sisters all have them. My nine nieces and nephews light up my life. I love when I get to spend time with them.

But mini golfing with Nicholas and Claire is a disaster. They both want the same color ball, and when I warn them that it'll be hard to tell theirs apart, they look at me like I'm an idiot and assure me that they'll remember where their individual ball lands. That works out for about four holes, and on the fifth, they devolve into a screaming match. Claire insists hers is the one closer to the hole. Nicholas is sure it's his. I had been, admittedly, looking at my phone and hoping to hear from Belle, so I have no idea whose ball is whose. Naively, I had assumed they were old enough to keep track of their golf balls if they had promised to do so. I collect the balls and call a redo, which makes neither of them happy, but we are at least able to finish the game.

Luckily, the course is nine holes and not eighteen, so we're only miserable for the last half. I may have been dumb enough to let them play with the same color ball, but I'm not so much of an idiot that I would win either, so I come in dead last by design. Claire beats Nicholas by one point, and he spends the entire ride home grousing about how, if I had believed him at hole five, he'd have won.

So, when we get home and they both grab their respective tablets and retreat to their rooms, I don't have it in me to enforce any of Annie's screen time rules. I'm fun Uncle Mike, not a strict parental figure. They can have at it.

I flop on the couch and check my phone again. Nothing. I don't know what I expect; we both decided it was a fun night, and it was best if we go our separate ways. But would it be so bad to be friends? She's funny and unique. I wish I had seen that about her in high school instead of only seeing her dyed hair, dark lipstick, and black nail polish.

Funny how much I've changed. Those lips and nails are *hot*. I might have unlocked a new kink.

My thumb hovers over her name in my phone, but I ultimately decide to leave well enough alone. It was a great night, but I'm headed back to Indiana right after the town's Halloween fest. It's for the best.

Instead, I scroll a little ways down and tap my buddy's name. Trevor's face pops on my screen after a couple of rings. He must be at work, because the wall of mugs at his coffee shop looms behind him.

"That'd be a cool aesthetic picture there," I say by way of greeting.

"Yeah, we rearranged the mugs the other day to snap a few photos." He chuckles and runs a hand over the auburn stubble on his jaw. "They promised we were done with the thirst trap social media posts, but I have a feeling Emery is cooking something up behind my back."

Emery and Trevor met when she did a series of stories for her online magazine about his shop to help him drum up some business. The articles were my idea, actually, which I never miss an opportunity to remind them. It not only worked, but they fell in love in the process. Now, just over a year later, his shop is doing great *and* they just moved in together.

"With a jawline like that, who can blame them?" I tease.

Trevor angles his face and half-closes his eyes in what I assume is his rendition of a cover model pose, but he's so awkward that it just looks like he's got something in his eye. He holds the position for a second, then laughs at himself. "Anyway, how are you doing? How's Annie?"

"Annie is good." I sigh. "I'm fine."

"Is being home everything you hoped and then some?" he teases. Trevor and I go way back, so he knows how I feel about spending any amount of time in this small town. I call him at least once on trips back here, usually when I'm about ready to move to an earlier flight. Ironic, then, that this time I almost don't want to leave.

"It's been... interesting," I hedge.

"That sounds like there's a woman involved."

It's scary how well he knows me. I shrug. "Yeah, maybe."

"You want to talk about it?"

"Not really," I grumble. I do, but I'm not sure what to say. I like this woman, but I'm headed home in a week? Staying at Annie's and knowing she's only a few minutes' walk up the street is torture? I know staying away from her is for the best, but I don't want to? Anything I admit is going to make me sound like a sad sack, and there's no answer he can give me that'll help.

"Okay," he says as a bell dings in the background. "I've got to get going, but you know where to find me when you're ready."

We say our goodbyes. I drop my phone to the ground and lay on the couch, staring up at the ceiling. I'm going to have to strengthen my resolve to steer clear of Belle. That's the only option.

***

I last three days. Three whole days before I throw all of my resolve and common sense out the window, get in my rental car, and drive to Belle's house. I don't walk. If I walk, it'll take longer, and once I've made up my mind to see her again, I need to do it fast.

Plus, it's raining. I can't have the water messing up my hair.

When I get there, her car is in the driveway, which is a good sign she's home. I throw my car in park and run up to her porch. I bang on her front door, then shift back and forth between my feet as I wait. Impatiently, I raise my fist to bang again, but the door opens.

Belle is there, her blue-violet eyes wide and her lips parted slightly. She's wearing black leggings and a gray off-the-shoulder shirt that displays the top of her bluebell tattoo. Her dark hair is in a messy bun.

She's beautiful. I have to clench my fists at my sides to keep from grabbing her and pulling her to me.

"Indy," she says, surprised. "What are you doing here?"

"This is stupid," I blurt out, suddenly regretting not preparing something to say on my way over here. "I want to see you. And, I was thinking, if you want to see me, then we should. See each other, I mean." Not the most eloquent, but it'll have to do.

"Okay," she says simply.

"Okay?"

She shrugs her tattooed shoulder. "You're right. We're adults who enjoy each other's company. Let's... enjoy each other's company."

I have no idea what I expected, but there's a giddy feeling rising in my chest, and now I don't know what to do. Luckily, Belle chuckles and grabs the front of my t-shirt to pull me inside. She slams the door shut as she spins to face me, her back to it. I don't waste any time, claiming her lips with mine and pressing her against the wood. She arches into me as I circle my hands around her waist.

"I didn't come here only for sex," I say. It seems like an important thing to clarify.

"I know." She bites my bottom lip, and I groan. "But I'm good with having it if you are."

"Fuck yes," I practically growl as I lift her shirt over her head. She raises her arms to help me, then does the same. As she drags her nails over the ridges and valleys of my abdomen, I take in the sight in front of me. She wasn't wearing a bra, and with her breasts and tattooed shoulder on display, I'm helpless to do anything but worship her.

"We need to move," she says, her gaze meeting mine. Her eyes are dark with desire, and it's a heady feeling, knowing she wants *me*. "I don't need my neighbors hearing all the sounds you're going to make."

"The sounds *I'm* going to make?"

She rolls her lips together against a smile. "Mmm-hmm."

I tick up an eyebrow. "Okay then." Bending over, I grab her behind her thighs and throw her over my shoulder. "Where to?"

Her laughter echoes off the walls of the entryway. Whatever happens at the end of this week, I hope I never forget that sound.

"Bed," she commands.

"Yes ma'am," I respond in my best Texan drawl as I carry her to the bedroom.

"Oh, I could get used to that," she teases.

I kick open her bedroom door and throw her on the bed. She squeals as her back hits the soft mattress. Her smile is contagious; I can feel mine responding to it. Fun. This is fun. Even if that's all it is, I can live with that. Right?

Looping my fingers under the waistband of her leggings, I shimmy them off over her hips and throw them to the floor. My dick hardens further when I realize she's not wearing panties, either.

"Woman, do you not own underwear?"

"I was just lounging in my own house, minding my business, when you showed up out of the blue."

"Do you always lounge without panties?" I can't tell if that note in my voice is incredulous or hopeful.

Belle smirks up at me. "Maybe," she say coyly. "Now, strip. Fair's fair."

I can't argue with that, so I drop my pants and boxers. My hands land on her inner thighs, and she widens her legs easily for me. "Let's see who makes what noises, shall we?" I say before I sprawl myself out on the bed in front of her and lick up her center.

She tastes even better than I imagined, and when she collapses fully back onto the bed with a deep moan, I hum, satisfied. Her hips buck a few times into my face, and I fist my cock, pumping in time with her movements.

"Shit," she chokes out breathlessly. "Right there."

I use my tongue to circle her clit, then plunge it deep inside her. I'm rewarded with more whimpers as her hips move wildly.

"Oh. Mike, I'm going to—" She's cut off by the force of her own orgasm. Her body shakes, and her walls clench and unclench around me. I lap up her arousal, drawing out her pleasure as much as I can, until she relaxes into the bed.

I open her nightstand drawer and pull out a condom from the stash we used on Friday night. "This okay?" I ask.

She nods, her eyes hooded as she watches me roll it on. I grab her by the ankles and pull her so her ass is just touching the edge of the bed where I'm standing. With her ankles on either side of my ears, I line myself up with her entrance and slide inside.

Belle's arms reach above her head to grab onto the comforter there. I thrust again, watching her perfect tits bounce with the movement. A low, guttural moan escapes me when I'm fully seated, just as she sighs, her eyes rolling back contentedly.

"You're so tight," I say. "God, it feels good."

She flutters her eyelids open, those gorgeous eyes sparkling with mischief. She lifts one of her legs from my shoulder and crosses it over her other ankle. It has the effect of squeezing me even more, and I almost lose it right there.

"Dammit, Belle," I groan as my thrusts become more erratic. "That's amazing."

Her fists ball up tighter into the comforter as she squeezes her eyes shut again. "It's incredible for me too," she breathes.

"Open your eyes," I plead. She obliges, her eyelids flying open so she can watch me. I lean forward so my hands are resting on the edge of the bed on either side of her hips, forcing her legs to bend closer to her. She bites her bottom lip and moans, but never takes her eyes off of me.

"That's it," I encourage her. "I want to see those pretty eyes when you come for me again." I brace myself and lift a hand to cup her breast. I tease at her nipple, pinching and rolling the dark bud between my fingertips.

"Yes," she pants. "Harder. I can take it."

"I know you can, baby," I croon as I squeeze her nipple even harder. "You like that?"

She cries out her pleasure as she squirms underneath me. "Oh god. I'm close."

"I want it," I tell her. "I want to feel you come." I thrust hard a few times, and she comes undone around me. Her tight pussy hugs my dick, and it sends me over the edge with her.

We never break eye contact. Even as we're sweaty and panting and her legs are still resting on my shoulder, it's like we're locked together. When I eventually have to step away to dispose of the condom, it almost hurts to have to look away from her.

And that's about when I realize that I want to look at Bluebell Allen every day for the rest of my life.

If only I knew how that could be possible.

CHAPTER 14

BELLE

"Come on," I taunt into the phone as I look at my clothes laid out on the bed in front of me. "It's your last night in town, and it's the biggest event of the year in Ironwood Flats. I want to go, and I also want to spend time with you. Please come with?"

I realize I'm twirling my hair around my finger. Grimacing in disgust, I drop it. When did I become the type of woman who twirls her hair when she's talking to a guy?

"Why don't you go for a while, and then call me when you're back. I'll come over after," Mike says. I try to ignore the soft sound of clothes landing in his suitcase in the background.

We've spent almost every available minute together since he came over a few days ago. We even took Nicholas and Claire to see a movie so Annie could see her first few nail clients in peace. It was sweet, but I knew I couldn't let myself get used to it. Maybe we'll still talk for a while after he leaves, but I can't see any real commitment blossoming between us, as much as it disappoints me.

"But you'll be missing time with your niece and nephew if you do that. This way, you can spend time with them *and* me." I'm trying not to sound desperate, but I fear I'm toeing the line.

I can tell by his silence that he's considering this. I've found over the past few weeks that there's no one Mike loves more in this world than his sisters' kids, and if I have to use them to get him to come with me to the Halloween fest downtown, I will. Shamelessly.

My hall clock chimes four o'clock. The festival kicks off at five. "Come on, Indy. We're burning daylight here."

"God, you are so *Texan*," he says, but it's affectionate. Almost wistful, like he wishes he still were, too.

"Yup," I say simply. "Come on. I'll point out where all the scary things are so you'll be prepared."

"You don't think anything is scary," he counters.

"Because it's not."

"So, what are you going to point out?"

He's got me there. I consider before saying, "There are a couple of skeletons that will jump out at you. I'll steer you clear of those."

It's silent for a moment, then he grumbles again. I've got him.

"Fine," he says. "But if anything pops up suddenly, I'm leaving."

"I'd expect nothing less. You want me to pick you up?"

He hums, as if he's not sure he wants to say what's coming next. "I should probably go with Annie and the kids. Since it's my last night with them."

"Oh. Right. Okay, then. I'll see you there." I let him say goodbye, and then hang up before my voice can betray me any more than it already has.

One thing's for sure. I'm going to miss Mike when he's gone.

I try not to dwell on it too much as I get ready to go. The whole point of the last week was to enjoy each other while we can. And we've certainly done that. My cheeks heat at the memories of everything we've done on this bed. My heart aches at the sweet nothings he whispered to me as we fell asleep, limbs entangled and skin slick with sweat. My brain can't seem to understand that this has been temporary. He leaves tomorrow, and then my life will go back to normal.

Though, I can't help but wonder if anything will ever feel normal again.

I shake myself, as if it's possible to let these emotions out through my feet and fingers. It's not, but it'll have to do.

I get dressed as quickly as I can, opting for black leggings, a short-sleeved sweater dress, and my well-worn combat boots. Usually, the kids wear their costumes to these things, but the adults don't. I'm well aware that my normal clothing choices look costumey, but I'll fit right into the vibe, anyway.

When I'm as ready as I'm going to be, I leave my house and make my way downtown. A carnival has been added to the mix in one of the church parking lots, and the smell of fresh popcorn hits me as soon as I get close enough to it. Children scream as one of the rides dips precariously, then saves them at the last minute.

It takes me less than a minute to spot Mike where he stands next to Annie at a cotton candy booth. Claire hangs onto one of his hands like she doesn't want to let him go.

I know the feeling, kid.

As if he senses my eyes on him, he turns around. I wave, and his smile lights up the evening like a crescent moon.

Shit. I am in so much trouble when he's gone.

The deep breath I take in through my nose is laced with the scent of sickly-sweet, fried dough. I let it out slowly and make my way over to their little foursome.

"Hi, Miss Allen!" Nicholas perks up as I get closer, his painted-on dalmatian nose wiggling with excitement. "I finished that book. Can I get the next one on Monday?"

"Sure thing." I smile down at him, then turn my attention to Claire. "My, my. What a beautiful butterfly we have here."

She buries her face in Mike's side, her wings bobbing with the movement.

"Claire is having a little trouble with Uncle Mike leaving tomorrow," Annie chimes in.

"I understand," I say quietly, but I don't bother looking at Annie when I say it. I'm glued to Mike's warm, brown eyes, hoping that he understands what I'm trying to say. I don't want him to go either, even though I know he has to.

His eyes fall to the ground as he squeezes Claire a little closer to him. "Come on, kiddo. You want to do some rides?"

"You hate rides." Her voice is muffled by the fabric of his jeans. When she shifts her face, she leaves a trail of glitter face paint on his hip.

"I do," he says. "But I'd go on one for you, if you want."

She shakes her head, more of her glitter shedding onto his pants.

"I know what might be fun," I say slyly. She peeks out at me cautiously, intrigued. "Let's watch your Uncle Mike bob for apples."

"What? No," he says quickly, but Claire removes herself from his side with a giant smile.

"Oh, that *would* be fun." She hops up and down. "Will you, Uncle Mike?"

"But... water. My hair..." he protests feebly.

"Your hair's got enough gel in it to stay put through a little apple bobbing," I assure him.

He glares playfully at me. "I'll do it if you do it."

"You're on," I tell him. Claire leads the way to the apple bobbing station. We line up, and when it's our turn, we take our places at two barrels next to each other. Laughing uncontrollably, we each bob in the water like roosters, trying to catch the slippery apples with our teeth.

When our time is up, neither of us have caught anything, but we're both dripping wet. They hand us towels to dry off, but Mike uses his to loop around the back of my neck. He brings me in for a sloppy, wet, wonderful kiss. It's the first time he's even touched me in public, and by the way everything goes quiet around us, I'm sure the entire town is going to be talking about this by the end of the night. But I don't care. I wrap my arms around his waist and step closer.

He pulls away from me, then uses the towel to wipe off his hair. It falls in floppy waves over his face. He whines about it a little, but it's half-hearted. He's having too much fun to care, it seems.

With Claire placated and Nicholas ready to ride the Ferris wheel, Annie sweeps both kids off to the carnival for a while. Mike and I walk around the fair, sharing a pumpkin funnel cake and drinking from plastic cups of beer. Our shoulders brush together as we walk, and when we throw away the powdered sugar-covered paper plate from the funnel cake, he links his pinky with mine.

Mike wins me a stuffed dog from one of the carnival games before we meet up with Annie and the kids. When he thinks they're not watching, he finds every excuse to touch me. His hand at my lower back. His knuckles brushing my collarbone. A small kiss on my temple. A brush of my hair over my shoulder.

At the end of the night, Claire is practically asleep as he carries her to Annie's truck. He sets the little girl in the back seat. Annie eyes him up and down, then nods once to him. He takes me a few steps away and threads his fingers through my hair so he can kiss me.

It's a kiss that feels like goodbye. Like we're both trying to pour as much into it as we can. Annie will take him to the airport tomorrow, and that'll be the end of it. I'll never kiss Mike Page again, and I have to be okay with that.

When he pulls away from me, he peers into my eyes, as if I have any answers for the questions he's silently asking. Without a word, he smiles sadly and turns back to Annie's truck.

The whole way home, I try not to cry. But when I crawl into bed alone, I clutch that stuffed dog to my chest. It smells like smoked cedar, and I sob into its soft fur.

CHAPTER 15

MIKE

ANNIE WAITS ON THE sidewalk outside my terminal as I heave my suitcase out of the bed of her truck. My flight is early this morning, so we dropped off my rental yesterday afternoon. I gave each kid a kiss on their sleepy cheeks before one of her friends came to sit with them while Annie drove me to the airport. We figured it'd be easier on them if I said goodbye at the house.

As soon as I wheel my suitcase up over the curb, Annie is on me with a fierce hug. I cradle her head to my chest and rock her back and forth. She's not crying, though, which is a good sign. My tenacious, pain-in-the-ass sister is back on track. I'm glad I could come out and help her get there.

"I'm going to miss you, big bro," she says into my shirt.

"I'll miss you all, too."

She looks up at me. "You said goodbye to Belle?"

I nod, swallowing against the lump in my throat. "Last night."

Annie's lips thin into a tight line. "You should call her when you get back to Indiana."

And say what? Thanks for the fun time? You made Ironwood Flats tolerable? I miss you, and I want to come back? Nothing I say will make this any better, and we all know it. But Annie will just pester me until I agree with her, so I say, "Okay," and leave it at that.

By the look she gives me, she knows I'm full of shit, but she lets it go. "Fly safe, okay? See you at Lindsey's for Christmas?"

"Yep. Love you, Annie." I kiss the top of her head, give her one more squeeze, and enter the airport.

Security isn't too bad this early in the morning, and I find myself at my gate with about an hour to spare. Great. An hour to sit here and contemplate all of my life choices that have brought me to this miserable moment.

Instead of wallowing, I call Trevor, intending to let him know that I'm getting on the plane soon and confirm that he'll be there to pick me up on the other end.

But when he sees me, his first thing out of his mouth is, "What's wrong?"

"I'm fucking tired," I say half-heartedly. "It's early, and I barely slept." It's not entirely a lie. I tossed and turned all night, thinking about Belle. Leaving her was like putting socks on a rooster, as my dad used to say. The night with her at the Halloween fest was magical. The stolen kisses, the surreptitious touches, being there with her for everyone to see. She felt like mine last night, if only for a moment.

The problem is, I want more of those moments.

"Is this about that woman?" Trevor's voice breaks me out of my reverie.

"Yeah," I admit. "I really like her."

"So, what's the problem?" he asks, as if he can't see the airport behind me in a clear signal that I'm about to be a thousand miles away from her.

I laugh humorlessly. "She's here. I'm there. Seems pretty self-explanatory."

Trevor scoffs. "You're both adults with jobs, I'm assuming." When I nod, he continues. "You work for a friend who lets you work remotely whenever you want. Get on a plane every so often and see her until you're sure this thing can work out, and then move."

"She doesn't want to do a long-distance relationship."

"Did you ask her that?"

"No," I say. "But we're in our forties. No one wants to do long distance. It never works."

Something on the other side of the screen catches his attention, and his eyes light up. There's only one person who can make his face look like that, and it's Emery. She must have walked into the room.

I've never been one to settle down. I briefly entertained the idea of finding The One after college but gave it up in favor of work and play. Until now, I haven't regretted that at all. But seeing Trevor make heart eyes at her makes me realize that I want that. Maybe he's right. Maybe it isn't out of reach.

He turns his attention back to me and regards me, considering. "Sometimes it works. You could be the exception to the rule. You never know until you try."

I huff, shaking my head. "Are you always this unfailingly optimistic?"

Trevor smiles. "It's something I've been accused of now and again." He pauses, then asks, "What are you going to do?"

I eye the woman standing behind the ticket counter. She looks bored. I guess I might as well give her something to do.

"I'm not sure yet, but I won't need a ride today. I'll call you when I figure it out."

He nods, looking proud. "Good luck, man."

"Thanks," I say, my heart beating hard in my chest. "I'm going to need it."

CHAPTER 16

BELLE

I'M IDLY WIPING DOWN tables at The Broken Spur when Old Man Peña comes in. The place is otherwise empty, but he takes his usual seat at the end of the bar, nonetheless.

I grab his beer from where I had set it on the counter. He prefers it closer to room temperature than it would be if it were straight from the fridge, so I always leave the first one out for him for a while before he arrives.

"What happened to you?" His voice is raspy, and his beard twitches with concern.

"Nothing," I say.

"You look lower than a gopher hole," he insists.

I can almost hear Mike saying, "God, you're so *Texan*," and I laugh wetly. I can't be surprised that he left. That was always the plan from the beginning. So why am I so sad?

"Is this about that man everyone saw you with at the festival?"

"How did you know?" I ask, moving behind the bar to stack the glasses out of the dishwasher.

Old Man Peña juts his chin at my shirt. Or, rather, Mike's shirt. He left his flannel at my house the first night we spent together, and I'm wearing it now. It still smells like him.

"He left?" he guesses.

I sigh. "Yeah. Back to Indiana, where he has a life and a job and friends and probably a million women just waiting to be with him."

He hums noncommittally and takes a sip of his beer. Swallowing loudly, he says, "Do you love him?"

I practically choke on my own saliva. I cough a few times, thumping my chest to clear it. "What the fuck? Where did that even come from?"

Unphased, he shrugs a shoulder. "I don't know. That's how it goes in the movies. I thought that's what I was supposed to say."

A laugh bubbles up out of me as I shake my head incredulously. "I don't know. I haven't really known him long enough to be able to answer that."

He looks at me with understanding, then takes a big gulp of beer and lets out a belch. Leave it to Old Man Peña to really drive a moment home.

"But you'd like to know him better. And fall in love." He says it like it's not a question. And it's not, I guess. He's right.

"Yeah," I admit. "I would have liked the chance."

"I hope you get it, then," he says simply, then turns his attention to one of the televisions behind the bar. Conversation over, I guess. And I don't feel any better about any of it. If anything, I feel worse.

The afternoon wears on. Patrons come in and out. The terrible Halloween playlist is still crackling through the speakers, even though Halloween is over. Eventually, I just unplug the MP3 player and turn up the football game. We hit a lull, and I start cleaning out the soda machine for something to do.

My back is to the door, and I'm on the other side of the bar from it when it opens and closes. "I'll be right with you," I call from where I'm crouched under the bar. I hear whoever it is take a seat as the torn leather squeaks underneath them.

"Well, well, well," the newcomer drawls. I go completely still. I glance up at Old Man Peña, but he's glued to the game and completely stone-faced.

Thanks for the help, Old Man.

But it can't be Mike. He's landed in Indiana by now. This is just wishful thinking. It has to be. I stay where I am to let my heart calm down.

"If it isn't Bonnie Bluebell Allen, as I live and breathe," the newcomer says.

And that's when I'm sure. I leap up and whirl around to face Mike Page, sitting at the bar, looking as calm and suave and gorgeous as ever.

"Mike," I say. "How... What..."

His smile stretches wide across his face. "I delayed my flight."

"For how long?" I ask.

"Two weeks. I'd have come here sooner, but I had to wait for another rental car. And I checked into a hotel. Annie would kill me if I stayed with her for that long—"

"Why?" I cut him off breathlessly.

His smile falters just a little. "For you. I mean, if you want. I do. Want to spend more time together, that is. Maybe see if we can give this thing between us a real shot."

I gape at him. "Seriously?"

"Yeah." He grows earnest, his grin completely falling. "I walked away from you once, Belle. I don't intend to do it again."

My hands fly to my face, covering my mouth as I laugh. "Oh my god. This... yes. Yes. I want that." Tears prick at the corners of my eyes.

"Can you two kiss and get it over with so I can get back to my game?" Old Man Peña says.

I narrow my eyes at him and shake my head, but Mike stands and comes around the bar. He wraps me in his arms.

"Nice shirt," he says.

"Thanks. I stole it from a guy."

"Looks better on you, anyway." And, with that, he kisses me deeply, right there behind the bar of The Broken Spur.

When we part, he laughs and says, "I'm happy as a hog in mud."

I bark out a laugh. "That's the most Texan thing I've ever heard."

He winks. "I'm trying it on. What do you think?"

"Needs work," I say. "Luckily, you should have some time to figure it out."

"*We* have some time to figure it out," he corrects.

Old Man Peña reaches over the bar to grab himself another beer. "And then they lived happily ever after," he mutters. When we both look at him, confused, he says, "What? That's what they say in the movies."

Maybe he's right. Maybe we can live happily ever after. For now, I'm glad to have the chance to find out.

EPILOGUE

MIKE

"And with that, the spooky night was over. Or was it?" I finish reading to the group of elementary school students sitting in front of me in the Ironwood Elementary library. Turns out, when you read aloud dressed up in a costume that makes you look headless, the kids pay rapt attention. So much so, that I've done this story time at the school every week in October. This is the last one, as the school's Halloween festivities are this weekend.

One of the children raises his hand. "Monster Mike," he says before I can call on him. "Can you read another?"

I look up at Belle, who is seated behind the group. She claps her hands and stands. "Unfortunately, you all have to go back to class now." The kids—and some of the teachers who had been watching from the back of the room—groan. "I know," Belle commiserates. "But Monster Mike will be back tomorrow for the haunted house, so be sure to come see him then."

Some of the kids come up to hug me, which makes Belle wince. Somehow, I found the one thing that creeps her out, and it's me holding my own head. When the library has cleared out, I lean in for a kiss, but she backs away.

"No way in hell." She puts her hands up in front of her and turns her cheek. "I'm not kissing your disembodied head."

"Why?" I tease. "Are you scared?"

"I'm disturbed. Go change."

I take a few steps toward her, puckering my lips. "Come on, Bonnie Bluebell. Plant one on me."

"Absolutely not," she says firmly, but her voice is filled with laughter.

"Fine," I roll my eyes. She shudders at the expression, and I laugh. "See you at home?"

"Yes." She grins then, and it changes her whole face. "But you better have your head back on your shoulders when I get there."

"Yes ma'am," I drawl on my way out the door.

It took us the better part of the year to figure it out. We tried the long-distance thing for a few months, but that was hard. The flights took a toll on our sleep patterns and our bank accounts, and being apart was excruciating. Eventually, I set up some fully remote work, said a tearful goodbye to my friends in Indiana, and came back home. I moved in with Belle in June.

I walk into our house and shed my costume. After cleaning myself up, I set about getting out the ingredients to make pumpkin bread. I call Trevor while I do it so he can walk me through how to make it perfect. Emery pops on the screen to wave at me about halfway through the call, and even though I miss them both, they have each other. Things are good. Really good.

After I get the bread in the oven, I hang up with Trevor. When Belle comes home an hour or so later, she takes a whiff of the air.

"Something smells good," she remarks as she kicks her boots off by the door.

"I made you pumpkin bread," I tell her.

"That's my favorite!" she exclaims.

"I know," I say, and then I kiss her deeply. She presses her body into mine, parting her lips for me so I can explore her mouth with my tongue.

She breaks the kiss, and I try to follow her. Shaking her head, she lays her palms on my chest. "Nope. I want to try this pumpkin bread first."

I lead her into the kitchen where she doesn't even bother with a knife. She just grabs a hunk of it and puts it in her mouth. "Ohmygod," she groans. "This is so good. Give me a latte, and I can die happy."

"I'll make you one," I offer, but she shakes her head.

"Maybe later," she says. She kisses me again, deeper this time, tasting of pumpkin and spice.

When we're lying in bed that night, planning for the upcoming Halloween festivities and digging into the pumpkin loaf with forks as it rests between us, I watch as her face lights up with a grin. She smiles so easily now, with me. She's my everything. And though it may have taken me twenty-some years, I'm so glad I finally found my way back home.

It seems Old Man Peña was right. We did, in fact, get our happily ever after.

Want more from Mike? Check out Common Grounds, available on Kindle Unlimited and anywhere paperbacks and audiobooks are sold!

Can a lifestyle reporter and a coffee shop owner find love brewing between them? Or will their blend be too bitter to succeed?

Emery Darlis hates her job. She's a journalist stuck writing feel-good local stories for a web magazine, and she's grumpy about it. In fact, she's going to burn out quickly if she doesn't get to write something more interesting soon.

Trevor Kovacic's coffee shop is failing. It's the place that houses all the memories of his family, and it's got two months, tops. He's trying to stay positive, but he needs a miracle.

Emery and Trevor have nothing in common. That is, until they share an unforgettable one-night stand.

They never expect to see each other after that, until Emery makes a bold bet with her boss to write a viral feature, and they end up face to face. Again.

Desperate to win and intrigued by Trevor's situation, Emery pitches a series of articles about his shop. They'll have to work together, but that should be easy... if they can each stop thinking about that one, passionate night.

If you love dual point of view, grumpy/sunshine books where he falls first and they both fall hard, don't miss this standalone romantic comedy. It will have you laughing out loud and crying tears of joy on an emotional journey to a happily ever after.

A Note About Setting

Ironwood Flats, Texas and Baker's Grove, Indiana are not real places. I tried to keep both settings as realistic as possible while also keeping them completely separate from any real place. Any likeness to real towns are purely coincidental.

***

Not ready to leave Ironwood Flats? Sign up for Allie's newsletter for free bonus chapters and behind-the-scenes content at https://alliesamberts .substack.com.

ACKNOWLEDGEMENTS

THIS BOOK WAS WRITTEN quickly, but it was only possible because it was a team effort. I have the most amazing team of people in my corner. For this one, especially, I leaned heavily on my support system.

I always start by thanking my husband, and I'll do it again because he's my number one fan, supporter, confidante, sounding board, and partner. When I said, "I think I'm going to write this quick novella," he didn't even hesitate. He just said, "DO IT." So I did. Thank you. You're my favorite. I love you.

Without Taiko Bennett, I would never have even had the idea to do this. I know you were probably joking when you said I should rapid-publish a Halloween novella, but thanks for lighting that fire. This was so fun, and I'd never have tried if you hadn't mentioned it in the first place.

Thanks, also, to Cait, Lexi, Jillian, and Hannah who not only put up with my approximately 1,237,384 messages about this book, but who also read, critiqued, and helped edit chapter-by-chapter as I wrote. It was so cool watching you read in real-time. Thanks for chasing any lingering doubt away.

To Team Mike aka my Hype Team aka my Enablers, thank you for putting up with approximately 3,482,398 more messages about this thing as I worked through the kinks, and we prepared for how to promote it. To April, Ashley, Catarina, Courtney, Hana, Hope, Jen & Victoria, Kae, Kathy, Kayla, Laura, Leah, Lindsey, MC, Mindy, Sarah, Sarah, Sarah (no, that's not a typo!), Sav, and Trish & Ash—thank you from the bottom of my heart for not only enabling my chaos, but believing it can result in something worth reading. Thanks, especially, to Kayla and MC with the Team Mike t-shirts. I'd better be seeing those again, soon.

A giant thank you to my agent, Katie Monson at SBR Media. Thanks for helping me bring these stories to new readers! It has been a joy to work with you.

The biggest thank you of all goes to my cover designer and friend, Lorissa Padilla. When I texted Lorissa asking her if she had any Halloween pre-made covers, she said she did, and then she re-drew the entire dang thing to fit my characters. She went above and beyond on this cover, and it shows. Not only that, but she did it fast! Thank you, Lorissa, for sharing your amazing art with me, and for leaning into the fun.

Thank you to my family and friends who probably won't even know I wrote this until it's out in the world. Since I was little, my mom, dad, and brother have been listening to me tell stories, and now, along with my sister-in-law, they're cheering me on as I write some that are ~~a little~~ a lot more grown up.

And last, but not least, thank you to my readers. These books simply don't exist without you. Thank you for reading my words, loving my characters, and enjoying my work. It truly means the world.

ABOUT THE AUTHOR

Allie Samberts is a romance writer, book lover, and high school English teacher. She was voted funniest teacher of the year for 2023 and 2025 by her students, which is probably her highest honor to date. She is also a runner, and enjoys knitting and sewing. She lives in the Chicago suburbs with her husband, two kids, and dog. You can follow her on Instagram @alliesambertswrites, TikTok at @alliesamberts, sign up for her newsletter at alliesamberts.substack.com, and get other updates at www.alliesamberts.com.

Also By Allie Samberts

Leade Park

The Write Place

The Write Time

The Write Choice

Standalones

Common Grounds

Love Out Loud

Novellas

Pumpkin to Talk About

Christmas by Design

Love in the Time of Conversation Hearts (with Hannah Bird)

A Holly Jolly Romance

Coming 2026 from Page and Vine

Not a Strong Enough Word

Not on the Same Page

Not the Way it Ends

Stay up to date on new releases and grab some bonus content! Subscribe to Allie's newsletter at https://alliesamberts.substack.com

www.ingramcontent.com/pod-product-compliance
Lightning Source LLC
Chambersburg PA
CBHW030010010826
48973CB00009B/2742